The
American Way

CASEY DURAN HOLMES

Order this book online at www.trafford.com
or email orders@trafford.com

Most Trafford titles are also available at major online book retailers.

Printed in the United States of America.

ISBN: 978-1-4907-3695-2 (sc)
ISBN: 978-1-4907-3693-8 (hc)
ISBN: 978-1-4907-3694-5 (e)

Library of Congress Control Number: 2014909541

Trafford rev. 05/29/2014

North America & international
toll-free: 1 888 232 4444 (USA & Canada)
fax: 812 355 4082

Dedicate

I wanna dedicate this book to all the families in the projects who struggle everday, living to make there ends-meat. To all the single mothers who are raising their kids on their won, "Don't worry" there will be better days and a better life, just hold on and be strong.

Thanks

I wanna thank all my family, friends, and love ones who believe in my thoughts and dreams, who encourage me to follow my goals, who told me to never give up and never get discourage, I just wanna say thanks and to my street mamas, my street brothers and my street sisters much love to my street family, "ya'll know who ya'll are" keep ya head up and smile for me.

"Star is born"

We are born with a qualification skill,

To help us disregard to conquer the world and build,

A better life, chances and days,

With better solutions, situations and better ways,

  Everybody is born a star.

By: Casey Holmes

Prologue

As we walk down the street contemplating and waiting for the adventure to come as we all think of the new trade we develop as, "thieves", some will look at it as a way to make money, some will say coma is a motherfucker, we though, we don't know what we doing it for, we just some bad ass kids who parents is either at work or at work smoking dope or selling the shit but, either though we was bad we didn't have much to lose living in the projects and coming home aint shit in the refrigerator or like majority of us" without shit period". I mean absolute nothing but a roof over our heads. That's, why we plotting now on our new trade of steeling but, we just call it steeling from the rich and giving back to the poor oh, don't kid ya self we don't steel from our people we Ashley walk or maybe sometimes catch the bus to those neighborhood we called the boonies our definition is = a better place then we live. As we think "I hope we don't get caught", I wish we can live like this", and fuck this shit". I'll mind frame was made up, we was determine to have something especially when you come home with or to nothing so, we took it. We all knew it was wrong cause, we all knew wrong from right but, thinking of the way we was living, we felt like we didn't have no choice and we knew the choices we made will one day come back to haunt us in the long run but, our mind frame right then was

"Fuck it"

CHAPTER ONE

"A Star Is Born" ....

I T ALL STARTED IN THE year of 1981 October 25, to be exact when a women name Joanna was in birth with her third child with a man name Joe. Joe was a good man when it came down to his family he been with Joanna for as long as the first two kids was in the world, Brandon was the first son a "handsome fellow he was", who was now 5 years of age and Ebony a beautiful daughter who was now 1 years of age was the perfect family I mean everything was going well until Joanna was having her third child who they named ather Joe but, something went wrong with Joe ather 4 years had pass I heard the man got around the wrong person and started smoking weed but a friend of his lace a joint they was smoking with some crack or PCP and Joe mind was never right from then on. A lot of things started to go wrong Joe just started tripping a lot not about his family but whatever Joe friend put in that joint that day fuck his whole mind frame up, he couldn't take the pressure of family or friends anymore so Joe left Joanna and 3 kids by their selves. Brandon was 9 going on 10 and Ebony was 6, Joe Jr. was going on 5 and barley knew the nigga anyway, Ebony a course was dady lil-girl but, Brandon, I can say it effected him more out of all of us cause he was use to his mom and dad being together and when Joe left, Brandon heart went with it so, every time Joe came around it was always Ebony and Joe Jr. who seen him. Joe Jr. barley knew him and was trying to understand this was his dady, Ebony adored him and Brandon never was present when his dad came around his mind was like he didn't have no dady and that made him the Black sheep of the family. Joanna, thank God she was a strong black women cause she move on and was destine to make sure here family

3

was gonna be o.k. regardless, with a little struggle she did just that at the same time, hoping that God will save her family.

Joe Jr. was the average heather lil-boy but his mind used to race a hundred miles per hour at a early age and that made a real bad case of studering, "I mean" he try so hard to express his self by talking but, he used to speak so fast that he couldn't even get one word out so, that kind of made him a more to his self kid growing up. It used to be hard though for Joe jr. when he first started school a lot of kids use to laugh at him a lot but, he was a very competitive kid and one of the best at all sports activities and that made him popular so kids might laugh but they never tease cause one thing he did have was a bad attitude and kids knew he get angry a lot, them or the teacher didn't want him to get mad cause he will hit fast, I think that why his mom nickname him Boogie ather the famous boxer and since he fought a lot that was like the best name for him cause he didn't play about being tease and that started a bad behavior problem that went with him his whole life. Joe jr. was more fascinated with woods maybe because it was a place that he could explore and a place he could be alone and didn't have to worry bout nobody. A place where people didn't exist and a place that his mind could race off in his world and nobody would ask him what he was thinking a place he felt safe, comfortable and more at home then home it-self, a place he knew would always be easy to find and a opining to go in, it didn't matter where he was, where they was any and every giving chance he had he went to the woods and he love every bit of it. In the first red bricks apartment they stayed was somewhere on the west side of Atlanta was the first place he met a white kid name Henrey. Henrey maybe was a little older then Joe jr. and I know it was the first white kid he ever met or even seen cause, when Joe jr. use to go to school he didn't see nothing but black forks and he never seen Henrey there but, when he got home Joe jr. ran straight to Henrey house and waited for him to come out side to play. Henrey was one of the craziest white boys I knew, well the only one I knew at the time and his fascination of the woods made my fascination grow even wilder, Henrey was the only kid who had a arson of fake guns that look more real than the real things I mean the boy had a fucking rocket longer something I never seen before real or fake I mean he had 38's,9's, 45s, AKs, rifles, knifes, holsters I tell ya and every fucking thing looks real as hell so we load up whatever we can carry and off to the woods we went looking for bad guys. Sometime we split up with walkie talkies and search the whole area I mean we always found knew places to go and check out when we left the apartment we stay gone damn near for 4 to 5 hours at a time it was a fun time playing with Henrey building forks and club houses in the woods and playing war it was one of the best times in Joe jr. life it was "awesome". Henrey was the only kid who I hung with at the time I mean I never really have many friends at the time except Henrey and a good friend he was. I remember when I was about 7 or 8 Henrey and I used to walk down the street sometime to a subdivision and it had the huge houses I mean big. I used to see things like this on T.V. and it was right down the street from where we lived. Anyway there was one house though that stood out from all of them it was so big and nice that I had to walk pass it damn near every day just hoping one day that I could live there and always telling myself that I would have something like that so my fantasies and my dream world started to hit me at a early age, and I knew whatever I did in life to stay focus on my dreams but my dreams got even colorful when one day my mom had a man name Greg to come by to visit, see Brandon, Ebony and me use to play bingo when we use to go out of town for our family reunions that's another story but, anyways our bingo was cars and we all look out the window at the cars that go pass and whoever say bingo first that was they car acourse Brandon since he was the oldest knew more bout nice cars and he use to win but every time he did say bingo I use to say it to I wanted the same one my brother pick so that got me fascinated with cars. So Greg pulled up in this candy apple red Cadillac with white leather seats and gold rims that damn near blinded me. I didn't know what this was called but, I wanted something like that so now my dreams are filled with big houses, nice cars, luxury, exotics and class and I wanted a part of it but, one thing I knew for me to have things like what I was dreaming and seeing only Hollywood stars have I knew I have to become a star and a star I was destine to be.

Bingo!!

"Ghetto Child"

As we live in a isolated, Drug related area

With people on the outside are, So afraid and scared of us

While never looking at the trials, Tribulations, problems of others'

The communities we live in, Disregarding our family, friends and mothers

If we are born in a world of low income, Well-fare with so much poverty

With no jobs, low education, with a struggle to provide food to eat

So acourse majority of the population, Gonna be bucking and wild

That's why we are the bricks behind the fence, known as the "Ghetto Childs" . . .

By: Casey Holmes

CHAPTER TWO

"GHETTO CHILD" . . . .

I N THE SUMMER OF 87, my mom Joanna finally, I guess got the courage enough to divorce Joe I think it what made him even come around less and less. Then it got to the point that he just stops coming around all together. Then she marry Greg who got us to move to his neighborhood. It was a big change for me cause I didn't want to leave Henry I mean he was my best friend but, I didn't have a choice anyway so, here we is on the South West Atlanta going to Greg side of town called the Westside. The apartments was a very crowded for a small community but, it was more kids and people outside all the time and all times at night, I mean you would think that nobody slept at all. Oakland city was the city and Demark was our street we stayed on. Greg who is now my step-dad knew everybody and everybody knew him, that's why everybody respected us cause of him, "I mean" he was the nigga in the hood and everybody wanted a piece of what he had because he was one of the biggest dope-man around and everybody love him, truthfully, I started to look up to him as my dad so I started to love him too. I never remember growing up with my brother and sister and when we move over to Demark it seem like I never seen them much. My brother Brandon used to always be up the street hanging out, cause he could and my sister Ebony used to always be with my mother friend Sara who use to keep her a lot and me, since I wasn't old enough to do nothing, I had to either stay in the house or go to my grandparents house on Martin Luther King it was cool though cause I got to play with my other cousins who stayed there.

One day on Demark as I sat in the house with my moma as I sat there watching TV, I heard a hard knock on the door and a women yelling and cursing, so I stood behind a wall and waiting for my moma to open the door. She went to the door, "who is it" she said. Then the lady outside said "Bitch opening this motherfucking door for I can beat ya ass bitch", bout that time a crowd started to pile up out-side just waiting to see what gonna happen. I seen my moma turn around and look at me with so much rage I was scared, then she turn around went in her room and put her shoes on and march right back to the door, peek out the window, the lady still cursing and knocking on the door she turn back to me, Boogie, "go to ya room," I didn't move" then she open the door bout this time the whole hood was out there. I see Greg trying to tell the lady to go bout her business when my mom open the door, then she said to my mom "bitch you fucking with Greg" he's my man" Greg told my mom just closed the door Joanna" but, she didn't she just stood there and I stood there too. Greg tried to tell the lady to go but, she would not listen, then turn around and started walking toward my moma and said, "bitch I finto beat ya ass" I never seen my moma jump on somebody before, the lady word didn't even get out good, my moma hit her dead in the middle of her face and the lady fell straight to the ground, it was like a one hitter quicker but my moma didn't stop there she jump on the lady and started to beat her more driving more and more punches in her face, everybody knew the lady was knock out but my moma didn't care. All I heard was my moma saying" if you ever come to my house again I will kill you, with every blow, then Greg pulled my moma up a push her in the house, don't know what happen to that lady but she didn't knock back on our door again. The next day everything was back to normal like nothing ever happen but, didn't nobody come back to my moma about it and we never heard anything else about it and nobody dared came back to comfort my moma Joanna about Greg again. She gains her respects from the hood and earns her stripes.

My step-dad was one of the coolest niggaz ever, since I was the only one who couldn't go anywhere, he started taking me places with him. Like to the store, his friend houses and to make runs. One time I was posted up at the store with him and his buddies, I was just standing there watching them drink beer and he gave me a swallow it was so hot that I didn't care what it was it was so refreshing and nasty I drunk damn near half of it, it was a tall 24 can with a blue bull and it had me feeling so good that was the first time I had a drunk of beer. Then I just started going everywhere with him. One time I was with him at one of his buddies house and a fight broke out, all I heard was one of his friend telling another one of his friends something bout "Who the fuck you talking too". I'm thinking they was playing cause everybody was sitting around playing cards and drinking beer, then the other dude was like "fuck you nigga" he said. Jessie the first dude was like 5'5 an 160 pond and the other dude Mark was like 6'5 350 but, Jessie wasn't gonna let his size intimidate him, Mark said "nigga I'll kill you" and started walking out the door, we was at Jessie house, so he got up ran to his room and came back with a sawed off shot gun and ran out the door ather Mark, everybody told Jessie to just chill out but, Jessie wasn't hearing it. As he caught up to Mark, Jessie said "what you say nigga" Mark turn around not wanting to fight his friend that he known all his life just stood there waiting for Jessie to get closer. Seeing Jessie running towards him with one hand behind his back, Mark said Jessie I don't even want too fight with you—all his words didn't even get out good. Jessie pulled the shotgun aimed it at Mark at first he had it up at chest level, then Mark said "you gonna kill me now", that when Jessie lowered the shot gun to Mark right leg and fired. It was like the loudest noise I herd in my life, then all I seen was Mark right leg disintegrated in mid air, at first I don't think Mark even knew his leg was gone, then he fell, and blood was everywhere. Jessie stood there for a moment staring at Mark and he said "don't ever hurt my life again, then another friend of both grab the shot gun out of Jessie hand at first he didn't let go then he release it, his friend yell somebody call the ambulance and he ran jump in his car with the shot gun a rode off everybody was shock and stood there for a moment but, I guess somebody called cause they came like 10-15 minutes later but I just heard my step-dad called my name "Boogie" I was stun so I didn't hear him the first couple times then he said "Boogie" I broke out of my stance and ran to him he took me to the car and yell to his buddies 'I got to go before the police get here", at first I didn't know why we had to go cause it wasn't like he had anything to do with it but, I realize that he was still hot cause he had dope on him and in the hood don't nobody get busted cause nobody dared snitch on nobody that was the code of the streets. Maybe a week later, we went back to Jessie house and guess who was there Mark with one leg walking with crashed drinking beer playing cards like nothing happen. Didn't nobody mention it or talk about it," if they did", it wasn't in the presence of them two or maybe to their selves but, nothing else wasn't said. Mark never told the police who shot him,

I think he told them he didn't know, so the case was dead and Jessie never got arrested. I guess that was the life they choose for their selves, 2 months later Jessie got shot and killed, people say Mark had something to do with it but nobody really knows. My mom tried to keep her kids in church a lot and I used to hear the preacher say "If you lived by the sword you die by the sword". And the hood "motto" was "If you live by the gun, you die by the gun", So I guess that what happen to Jessie. That was the first time seeing something like that just someone getting shot but, I told myself," it might want be my last".

I used to watch wrestling a lot on T.V. that used to be my favorite show, I used to all ways imitated the moves of my favorite wrestler like, Sting, The Atomic Warriors, Junk Yard Dog, Ric Flair, Lex Luger but, my favorite wrestler used to be the UnderTaker. One night they was coming to Atlanta and Greg told me he was gonna take me. I mean I was so ready for it I couldn't even sleep the night before so, when he got there to pick me up, when we made it up there, the arena was close, I was so disappointed, so he said "What we gonna do now" "I don't know", was it a question for me or he was just talking to his self. I wanted to see the Under Taker so bad in person; I just brush it off as we rode away from the Arena. Truthfully I didn't care I just was glad I was out of the house. I thought he was finta take me back to the house but, we went a different way so I straighten up in my seat and enjoyed the ride and the venture to come so I started to feel a little better cause I wasn't ready to go back home.

He rode to this other neighborhood as we rode down this dark street cause all the street lights seem like they was out of order but it didn't keep people from being out side and in the shadows and it didn't keep Greg from yelling out the window to everybody he seen yelling "a what's going on" "Our bee back", as people started to approach the car he never stop even when they called his name he never stop he just said "I'll be back", man he knows everybody and everybody knows him, I was thinking. As we rode on down the street he stop at one house told me he will be right back and lock the doors. Bout 5-10 minutes later he came back out with a couple bags, one he gave to me, one he threw under his set and the other one he kelp for his self. He said, "I got some steak sandwiches for us", so I took out a sandwich wrap in some aluminum foil some chips and 2 25 cent juices, man, that was one of the best sandwiches I ever had in my life it was um um good. We rode on to another hood, it wasn't like the hood we stay in now, they was more like our old apartments but, bigger I mean big. We rode through there and ended up in front of a house were people was gather around then he said "we finta go in here for a minute alright" I just shook my head, he didn't know I was just glad I wasn't at home right then. He grab that bag he threw under the seat and pulled out either a 9 or 45 and tuck it in his pants he said "Come on" so we got out of the car as I close the door I glance back at the clock it was 12:00 am. I was thinking to myself my mom gonna beat the shit out of me when I get home but, at the moment I didn't care.

As we walking up to the house people sitting around drinking and smoking and women half drunk and some them men and women look half dead. In the back yard there was some guys taking seats, steering wheels, tires, rims out of some cars, they even was taking the motors out at this time at night but everybody said what's-up to Greg as we walk up to the door to the house. I hear loud music, it was the Oldies. Greg knock on the door and a man came to the door look at Greg then look down at me then back up to Greg. The man name was Odis and I guess Greg already knew what Odis was thinking so he said "This Joanna son Boogie ather that he smile at me and said yall come on in the whisper in my ear and said "I'm ya uncle Odis. We step in and walk pass I guess it was the living room but it had tables everywhere and all of them was full with people playing cards, drinking beer, liquor and smoking cigar and cigarettes and it was foggy. As we walk pass to the kitchen it was more people in there shooting dice on the wall and two men was cooking something that stink real bad on the stove in a glass pot but, nobody didn't turn around to acknowledge us so, we kelp walking to another room where Greg told me to sit down in a chair so I did and him and uncle Odis sat in a couple chairs around a table. Now I heard the music go off and come back on with Marvin Gay all I heard was "Love and happiness" Then uncle Odis look at me and said "Boogie, close the door" I got up and close it. When I was turning around Greg was pulling out that other brown bag and put his gun on the table and handed the bag to Uncle Odis. He took out like 5 big stacks of money with rubber bands on them and gave Greg another brown bag then they got up Uncle Odis went somewhere and I followed Greg up stairs where some more people was but there was 4 rooms then Greg took out a key and open one door from the outside and walk in. The room was small but comfortable, Greg lock the door behind us and went to a table in the corner, I sat on the bed. He remove a big white brick like from the bag and broke it in half wrap on half back up and started to chop one half down banging it up in little brown envelopes. I didn't speak, he didn't speak we was like that I think for about a hour I don't really know cause I fell asleep and woke up when he shook me awake saying "Boogie come on" so I got up, the house was still the same when we left, before I walk out the door Uncle Odis said Boogie I turn around and he threw me a bag I look in to it and it was candy and cupcakes, I smile and said "Thank you Uncle Odis", he said "anytime". When we got back in the car, I look at the clock it was 4:00 am, I said my moma finta beat my ass I know it, then we rode off.

When we made it back to the house my moma wasn't even up and Greg told me to go a lay down he said "Don't worry bout ya moma, I got ya", so I took my bag of all my junk food that I receive all night and went to my room, took off my shoes got in bed and fell straight to sleep.

I woke up the next morning walk to my mom room, seen Greg and her still sleeping so I closed the door back. Made my way to the kitchen open the refrigerator and found nothing as usual, so went back to my room look in my bag from last night and grab a pack of cupcakes you know the two pack chocolate crème filled cakes with the string of icing on the top, look at the time it was 10:30 so I slept kinda late grab my last 25¢ juice and went outside and sat on the front porch. As I was opening my cupcake, the neighbors lil-boy and his lil sister came out the house, I think they was about 3 and 4 years old so I said "yall get back in that house", they enjoyed me and the lil girl who I think was the oldest said "cake" I got annoyed then but, I broke one in half and gave one to her and the other piece to her brother, both wearing no shoes and running noses. The little girl had on a dress that look like it was to big for her and the boy had on a sagging pamper that probably was filled with shit and piss cause it smell real bad, I was thinking why his moma or dady aint change that boy pamper. They eaten the piece of cake so fast I thought they had swallowed them, I felt bad so I split the other one in half and gave it to them, they couldn't really talk but the smile on the faces said thank you for them, then a voice called their names from inside their house and they ran back in there door, the little girl wave by to me then close the door. The hood starting to wake-up cause people starting to come outside, cars booming though with their radios loud, street walker starting to knock on street hustler doors looking for that wake-up, window start to open in other apartment to get fresh air inside. It was the average day in the hood what we called "The Getto Life". I wasn't ready for the getto life today, I was still tired from last night so, I drunk my juice went back to my room, jump in my bed and felled back to sleep.

"Hopes & Dreams"

As we hope and pray, That our dreams come true

Only the one's that is good, Never the ones that are sad or blue

So we struggle and fight, in a dramatic world of sleep

Waking up to another day, With a cold sweat and a bundle of weep

Now trying to hold back, The frustration, anger and tears

While still trying to succeed, For we can see better days and years

Determine to find out, What do these thoughts mean?

Still trying to stay strong and focus, On our hopes and dreams . . . .

By: Casey Holmes

CHAPTER THREE

"Hopes & Dreams" ....

J OANNA WAS THE TYPE OF mother who believed in staying strong for her kids and for her man. The pressure and the problems Joanna had, a lot of women would have been broke down but, Joanna wasn't weak and she was determine to make a better life for herself and her kids. Even when Greg came in the house with a drunken rage, and beat my moma up, I mean it was occasion that she even came out swollen face or lips but she never one time called the police on him. Then I think she started to realize, that wasn't the life she wanted to live for herself or her kids so, Joanna started to work, she even was working like 2 or 3 jobs at a time, we was happy for our mother but we started to see her less and less. So now I neven seen my brother and sister less and less. Brandon had a friend across the street but, he never came home anyway. Ebony stayed with our mother friend Sara and I stayed at my Grandparents house my dady side of family and we just never seen each other much at all, my moma and her kids, it was like we didn't even exist, but we did what we had to do for our moma. One time my Grandparents took me to jail and my moma was behind a glass window, I never seen my moma in a place like this I wanted to hug her but, I couldn't so I just sat there speechless and blank out from the world. I think she even said something to me but, I never said a word. Come to find out Greg got busted, the police kick in the door to our apartment and they lock her up too. Greg took all the charges so eventually they let my moma go. Greg was charge with trafficking cocaine and was sentence to 10 years and my moma was put on probation just for being around the drugs at the time. Now since Greg was gone, she had to work even harder to try to get us out the hood Greg brought us to. It was real hard for a single mother with 3 kids but she never led on to how hard it really was and we never ask. I heard moma one night say "O Lord, I hope and pray that my dreams stay positive and you keep my mind focus, my heart clean and my soul save in Jesus name Amen."

The mind is the Key and our source but, without knowledge;

It will become the death of us . . . .

Thoughts of Casey Holmes

Drive to move forward to build yourself a better future,

Because your past will always keep you in reverse . . . .

Thoughts of Casey Holmes

"Dope Boy Fresh"

With the Armani suites and gator boots

With the mink coats and gold ropes

Jerry curls, braids and finger waves

Kangoo hats and Dickies slacks

Nautica trunks and high heel pumps

Belly rings and demand pinky rings

Short miniskirts and Coggi purses

Starter coats and black lakes

Covers all stars and fly cars

This is a fashion statement, Who can look the best

Just being cool, From the head to the shoes

Is what you called, "Dope Boy Fresh" . . . .

By: Casey Holmes

CHAPTER FOUR

"Dope Boy Fresh"....

NE DAY OUT OF THE year, all the big time money maker go in together for the community and have a day called "Flood day", it when everybody put on the freshest gear and stunt for everybody and have a good time. We meet at the hood park over was Oakland city and chill with your friends and families, while someone crank-up the grill and cook hotdogs and hamburgers all day long for everybody. They have drinks and chips, beer for the grown up and recreation for the kids. Some of the grown up set up table and play card and dominos. People bring their pit-bulls to show off to theirs and who have theirs and be debating whose look the best, built up the best and whose the toughest. It's a day for everybody to show off, even the people who don't have anything; if you were hood you were there and were treated like hood. It was more of a day off from the block for most and a chill day for other and a fun day for the kids.

This was the first time I been to something like this, I mean everybody was there. I seen my brother, he was chilling with his homies from the hood. We came with Sara, since everybody knew her cause Greg was still lock-up. It was Ebony, Sara, moma and me. Soon as I seen by brother I ran straight to him. He was wearing Malcom X shorts with a black shirt and the Malcom X Jordans, his hair was a high top fade and some black looks that I couldn't even see his eyes but, I was glad to see him. "What's up lil brow" he said. "What's up" "Where you been" I said, he just smile then we started walking back toward moma them. As we walk toward moma I heard someone say "Yo Brandon" we both turned around and it was Reggie my brother friend from across the street. Reggie was a tall Red nigga who everybody called Red fa short. He wore all red

Addidas jump suit with a Red fur kangoo with the red and white addias and had on a big gold ropes around his neck that I only seen Cool Moe D and Run DMC wear on videos. My brother said "What up boy" then they dap each other up, then Red said to me "What up boy" I said what up Red then we walk on. When we got where my moma was I notice Uncle Odis, I was wondering why he was here but, everybody greeted him like he was part of the hood so, I guess he was. He was one of the flyest niggaz there. He had on Fasachi shirt that was red, purple, orange and crème, with the crème Fashichi pants, red and crème gators and a cream cowboy looking hat with a red and black feather sticking out, he had a little rope with a cross hanging from it and a nugget pinky ring with a nugget gold watch to match. He was sharp to the tee., him and my moma was bobbing there heads bout something so I waited to they was done, then he seen me and said "What up Boogie" I said What up Uncle Odis" then he said "You to big to give your uncle a hug" so I ran and gave him a hug" he push me back gave me a couple friendly pushing then another hug, then I ran off, hearing my moma yelling in the distance "Don't run off to far. There were women out there wearing nautical swim trunks, nautical t-shirts with some fresh clean reeboks all colors and there was some women with hair-dos that look like bee-hives on their head with sparkling pieces on them with gold chains, rings and bracelets on both arms and all fingers I mean they were blinging. One women had almost 10 earrings in one ear and the other one had just as many but, she was real pretty every time I get caught staring at her she wink her eye and smile at me, then I run off. Every once in a while I see the police circling the park but they never stop one did though but, I think he was doing paperwork then rode off.

As the sun was going down it seems like the park got crunker and liver, it really seems like more people started to come and came to see what was going on. It seems the party just started, and didn't look like anybody was leaving anytime soon either.

There was one dude name Jerry, now Jerry might was one of the coolest dudes ever. He pulled in a drop top chevrolet camprice, blue with the white leather and N,9's crome d's and I think the whole park got silence and stared at Jerry. He had three women one driving and all of them was pretty. When he open the door he pull a gun from under the seat and it disappeared in his suit somewhere. Then he step out he was in a all white Amani silk shirt and pants with white leather boots that look so clean you probably coulda ate off of them. His hair was jerry curls it wasn't to drippy or to dry, just the right amount of juice. He had on like 4 gold chain all different with different charms a gold watch on one risks and a bracelet to match his watch on the other. He had one diamond pinky ring that you probably coulda seen from here to the West-end on one hand and the other hand had a gold ring with a dollar sign and another one with a eagle. When he put his Amani shades on, when he smile, you can see his whole mount was gold, every damn tooth.

When the lady who was driven step out and came around she wore a white silk dress with white skraps around here legs staleg does a white mink coat that look like it was too hot for but, she didn't put on like it was. White pearl necklace, ear rings and the bracelets to match. Her hair was in a jerry curl just like Jerry but laid down on the side to form a jerry curl mohark but despite that she was stunning and beautiful. Damn near every kid ran pass me and rush up to Jerry with their hands out. I didn't because I didn't know him but my eyes did get big when he took out a wauld of money and started to peel off dollars and two dollars to the kids, he was saying "woo woo woo it enough for everybody and they kept coming. When he was done passing out money to the kids he started walking toward the crowd in the park, he look over and seen me under the tree and said "A lil-man, you don't want nona Jerry's money" I said "No", he said "come here lil-man" I look at him and put my head back down, then his voice seems like it got more offended and said again come here lil-man so, I started walking toward him, glancing around my shoulder to see my Uncle Odis looking at me so, I knew that everything was alright, still walking slow and glancing over at Uncle Odis. When I was in front of him, he said "you don't want none of Jerry's money" I said "no", then he put the whole wauld of money in my face and said "you don't want Jerry's money lil-nigga" I was so scared I slap the money out of his hand and turn to run when another hand grab my shoulder and spun me around, it was Jerry he said "you lil-muthafucka" then his other hand was coming up then down with a fist bawl, then another hand grab his, it was Uncle Odis. He grabs Jerry hand so fast and slap Jerry so hard, slob of spit come out of his mouth. I move behind Uncle Odis and he said Jerry you bad not ever raise "slap" your hand "slap" to this "slap" child again "slap" "slap" then reach under Jerry shirt and pulled his gun. Jerry said "Yo he didn't want to take Jerry's money" then Uncle Odis slap him a couple more times and said "Do you know who this kid is nigga "This my nephew" This is Greg son and when I tell him what you was about to do "slap", now blood started to come down his face and on his white suite Jerry said "Sorry "O" I didn't know" "slap slap", his words didn't even get out good. Now Jerry was saying "Don't tell Greg" with more fear in his eyes. Then Uncle Odis said "If you ever try to put your hands on him again I'll kill you myself, "you hear me" Jerry nodded his head in replay. Now everybody in the park was watching but, nobody said a word. Then Uncle Odis took my hand and walk me over to my moma. I glance over my shoulder and seen Jerry and the lady getting back in the car and pulling off, then everybody resume what they was doing. Uncle Odis pulled me to the side and said "That bad man want ever bother you again" O.K", I just shook my head in agreement. Then on, I knew it didn't matter how clean you was, you still can always get dirty.

Stay focus on the situation to come, sometimes the situation want emerge
Until times get hard but, when those times come around, stay strong,
Stay focus and believe with the faith in God; the only one who can bring
You out of the situation. Everything happens for a reason so, "Stay Focus" . . . .

Thoughts of Casey Holmes

The crome pistol pass, pose the same as a badge

Either manor women, Bone fare or sky mask

A money opportunity, In there eyes' is dollar signs and greed

Lay you down with guns drown in your face, Or tell "Get down on your knees!!"

As you plead, I don't have nothing. "Not know they already peep the scene

No more time to waste pistol whip to the face, As they search your house for cream

Your mind flash back wishing you had your gack, knowing that's how you shoulda open the door

While they search your house thinking you knock out, As they left you laying on the floor

Now your time running out, Waiting for the scene to play out

You done got caught slipping, Now strangers roam your house . . . .

"The Stick Up Kids"

By: Casey H.

CHAPTER FIVE

.... Stick Up Kids

I T WAS A HOT SUNDAY afternoon as Uncle Odis heard a knock a the door, he knew it wasn't business cause he didn't do business on Sundays it was like a chill day for him, the only day out the week he didn't do nothing and everybody in the hood knew it. "Who is it" as he yell through the door. "It's Pete" he heard the voice called back. He knew who Pete was a young nigga who been getting in trouble all his life his dad big Pete was serving life without parole for killing some dude who they say was trying to rob him but, everybody knew it was the other way around. As he open the door, "nigga what you want" my mom sent me over here, she wants a couple beers" he said. His moma was Vivian a known junky and prostitute in the hood who send her son on deliveries for her while she probably got a trick at her house. Looking behind him he had his boy Larry behind him. Odis said to Larry and "what you want nigga" Pete cut in he's with me Odis; you know this my role dog". It was something bout how Larry was acting looking around him and sweating so Odis said to Larry "nigga what's wrong with you" He said "nothing. Odis brush it off thinking these lil nigga probably just geek-up off of some coke or something so he let them in. told Larry to close the door as he was walking ahead of them going to get the beer for Vivian, saying to Pete "you tell ya moma that she know I don't do business on Sundays but I gonna make an exception for her today "he tell everybody that but, he don't never miss no money but he know it Sunday and he's the only one that got beer and liquor so he sold it anyway to certain people. He was at the refrigerator duck down in the door when he ask "what kind she want she know it gonna be extra cause it Sunday "he didn't get no response so he look up and Pete had a glock 9 to his face. Odis said "boy what you doing nigga" Pete said "close the door to the refrigerator and get down on your knees "odis said "what the fuck boy, this must be a joke" Then Pete said "I known you all you life now you gonna rob me" Pete said "shut up nigga" and slap him again with the pistol. Pete look around at Larry who was behind him shaking with fear and said "Pete let's get out of here, this wasn't good ideal man let go". Pete said shut-up nigga and pulled your gun out reluctantly Larry did. Pete said to Larry "nigga it done now we got to go all the way". We won't lived to see tomorrow if we leave now "Look watch him and I'm gonna search the house. Pete ran off and Odis said to Larry "Why yall doing this for "man" I know all your people Larry you really think yall gonna get away with this Larry. Larry said "shut up" and you can hear fright come out of his voice then he slap Odis in the back of the head with a weak sloppy blow and yell "Pete hurry up man let's go" no response so that made Larry even more nerves. Odis was playing like he was knock out but he could hear everything that was going on he didn't move cause he didn't want to get hit again so he layed still. He herd Larry again saying "Pete man hurry up" still no response. Then Larry said "fuck this shit" then his footsteps started to walk away going toward the other room where apparently Pet was. Odis knew this was his opportunity to go for his gun, he knew there was gun all over the place cause he stach them all the time under the couch "Yea under the couch" he said under his breath. He only had one eye cause the other one was close shut but he knew nobody was there with him so he got up and ran to the couch reach under it and grab a mosberaul shoot gun, he knew it had 8 shots cause he kept all his guns loaded to the tee and he didn't have to pump it cause he kelp one in the chamber. He started walking back to the door, Larry came out pistol pointing down probably thinking Odis was still laying there knock out, then he look up then seen Odis with the shot gun, he pulled the trigger. The buck shot hit Larry in the belly but before Larry hit the floor Odis pump another one in the chamber and fired again this one knock Larry whole head off his shoulder now Larry lay dioballdenated. When Pete heard the shot he was busy stuffing his pockets that he didn't even see Odis behind him with the shot gun then he turn around gun on the bed reach for it but Odis fire and knock him back against the wall. Odis pump another shell in the chamber and walk toward Pete he was still breathing, blood coming out of his mouth but he manage to say "Jerry Jerry sent me" "I didn't want to but he told me he would kill me" sorry Odis "Odis said "sorry Pete" then put the barrel to Pete head and pulled the trigger.

Odis head was dripping with blood and head had a headache out of this world but he had to get this shit clean up, he thought of the one person who could help him at the moment Bobby he pick up the phone and dial the number It only took Bobby 2 rings to pick up "Hello" Yea this is Odis he said "What's up Odis what ya need" "I need my carpet it was code for he need a cleanup, Bobby said "I'll be there in 10 minutes" Then Odis said "and another thing is you can go by the store and get some pain pills and some bandages "bandages was code for sticks "I'll be there in 10 minutes "Bobby said then hung up. Odis sat down on the couch and waiting for Bobby and tried to think about what just went down.

Bobby was a big dude, he was 6 feet tall and about 400 pounds he had his own Mortuary that he inherited from his father who inherited from his father and so on. He ran it well, still doing church services but his side job was the clean up man. He was a very humble person. I guess that's how you get when you been around dead people all your life. He ran a light business but he did side job for his hood.

Odtis heard somebody knock on the door, he grab his shot gun and went to the window, look out and seen Bobby he open the door. Bobby had on some overalls like he was going to paint but, you would wonder where did he get these overalls to fit him. He had a bucket in his hand and a paint chipper in the other. He seen Odis face and said "I told you about playing softball with no glove "he didn't laugh and Odis didn't see no hint of a smile, he walk pass Odis and said "what you got." Odis said "one in the kitchen and one in the back room". He open the front door waved the hurts he pulled up in and three men and a women jump out all wearing overalls and buckets. When they came in, he told one to pulled the car to the back and came back in the back door, he nodded and went. The other two he said "In the kitchen and the back bedroom "he didn't have to tell them nothing else they went pass Odis without even glancing his way and went to work. The woman told Odis to sit down and she examine his face she said "Yea you gonna need 10 stitches without no response she handed Odis 3 pain pill of 800 he took them then she started working on his face. Bout time the third guy came back in the other two was already hauling out the 2 bodies in big black bags and the other guy started cleaning up. Booby wasn't doing nothing but pointing here pointing there and just being the man in charge. When the lady got done with Odis face he notice there wasn't no trace of blood nowhere and the walls was clean and repainted even in the bedroom where the blood was on the floor it been cut out and replace. As Odis look around he didn't see nothing out of place, like nothing ever happen. Odis said "Bobby, what I owe you my man" Bobby said "Odis don't worry bout it you look out for me plenty of times free of charge "what you want me to do with them guys." "I don't want no trace of them to exist" Odis said Bobby turn to his crew and said "burn everything". That mean they was going in the furnace. He told his crew to go and do that now and he will be there later, he said something else to them then they left. Bobby turn to Odis but, first he grab a beer out the refrigerator handed Odis one and said "you don't mind coming back to the mortuary do ya" Odis said "Do I have a choice "Bobby said "No". They both sat in silent for a minute then Bobby said "so why in the hell did Pete and Larry try to rob you" I knew them niggas be up to no good" Odis was shock at first but "he said how you know it was them." You know I know everybody and bodies in the hood". With a smirk. Odis said "man I need another beer" Bobby went and got them hand Odis one. Then Odis explain to Bobby what went down, who sent them and what he had to do. Bobby never said a word but with a smirk on his face Bobby said "I'm gonna have a good business this year" Then he laugh a laugh that put a chill even in Odis but, he knew what Bobby was talking about.

Prepare, prep and deliver yourself from your surroundings,

It will take a lot of effort, adrenaline and ambition but,

Never forget that everybody will suffer downfalls but,

It takes a strong and wise person to overcome them . . . .

Thoughts of Casey Holmes

"Dreams"

Dreams have me scared, To wake up in the mist

So much anger of frustration, now I'm a mad man piss

Flipping the cards, That was somehow dealt

A full house of demons, In my heart somehow I wept

Asking myself, Why these dreams feel so real?

Waking up in a cold sweat, Now my eyes are feel with tears

Now tossing and turning, And can't go back to sleep

Afraid of the things, That always been hunting me, "In My Dreams" . . . .

By: Casey Holmes

CHAPTER SIX

"Dreams" . . . .

THE DREAM WOKE HIM UP in a cold sweat, he's head was ponding still from the blow from last night, he reach over the night stand grab three more pain pills that Bobby left him and the glass of water and gulp them. He look at the time it was 5:00 am Monday morning, he couldn't go back to sleep so he layed there staring at the ceiling for a couple minutes thinking about the dream he just had, it was more a nightmare, his whole world was upside down right now and he couldn't shake the feeling.

Odis knew that his business would be up and running by 12 noon but, he knew he couldn't run it so, he had to make other plans to keep his business running cause he had other business to take care of "Jerry". When he thought about Jerry he just got angrier and his head throb even more. He got up out of bed and went to the shower, the water actually made him feel better, he stood there with his eyes close for a second the whole dream didn't come back but flash backs of him laying in a coffin and him getting buried stayed the focus of the dream. Then the tomb stone it read here lies a real O.G. from the street Odis Gray, then he's eyes open and got out the shower. He got dress and was out the door before the sun came up.

Odis drove to Sam house and woke him up with some vicious knocks to the door he finally came to the door and said "who the fuck is it" "it's Odis, Sam open up", Sam still rubbing sleep out his eyes when he open the door and said "What the fuck Odis it's 6 in the morning . . . ." his whole sentence didn't even get out when he seen Odis face, What the fuck happen to you nigga" I got rob he responded" can I come in nigga" my bad man, you know my house is your house" Odis went in sat down,

"Is anybody else here" Barbara but she upstairs sleep" Sam sat down across from Odis with so much evil in his eyes Odis knew what he was thinking, he was thinking bout killing everybody who had something to do with this. See, Sam was a little older then Odis, he was 6'3" bout 200 pounds solid and was stronger than an ox. Him and Odis grew up together and always remain close, he was Odis right hand-man and Odis trusted him completely. Odis started telling Sam what happen and even though Sam just got up He was fully awoke now. When Odis got done narrowing everything down, all Sam said was I'm gonna kill that nigga "No Sam I'm gonna handle that personally "What I need you to do "anything Odis" Sam said. "Is run the Gambling house. "Odtis knew Sam knew how to run the spot and trusted him fully with his money and Sam was well respected in the hood and all he said was "Where you going" "Well ather I take care of my business with Jerry, you know it gonna be hot for me so I'm gonna go out of town for bout a year, just like a little vacation. Ya know what I mean "Sam said "Odis let me handle that shit, you know I got these Goons that will take care of that nigga and you wouldn't have to go nowhere "I know Sam but, this is personal and I just got to handle this myself. Sam didn't say nothing else about it, see Sam knew when to let it go but he was just mad for his friend Odis and was loyal to him and just didn't want to see his friend leave. Odis knew that but he didn't want nobody else involve and it was something he had to do alone.

Odis got up walk to the door, handed Sam a envelope with $5000 and said "You know what to do, everything there. You know it might crank up bout 12 so you might wanna get there early, I'll keep in touch with you on the up and up, "Odis open the door and before he jump in the car Sam said "be careful" Odis turn to his friend and with a lil smirk said "I'm not the one who need to be warn and with that jump in his car and drove off. Sam look at the car rode off until it turn the corner and told his self that he want see his friend for about another year and as a loyal friend," business will still be booming when he get back whenever that may be".

It was still early and he had one more stop to make before he handle his business and disappear. It was 9 now and he was hoping Joanna was home. Reluctantly her car was park outside so he knock on the door. She came to the door wearing a sweatshirt and jeans with no shoes. She immediately let Odis in. he sat down and said "I need to talk to you" she responded "What happen to your face" he said "a accident" she brush it off and said "What's up Odis" She seen so much violence in her life she knew not to pursue the issue. Before he was finto speak he seen Boogie standing there out of the corner of his good eye he turn and said so you just gonna stand there and not say nothing to your Uncle Odis, he ran and jump on Odis leg gave him a hug and said "What's up Uncle Odis" then look up and seen his face and said "What the fuck happen to you" It caught everybody off guard Joanna said "you better watch your mouth" he said "sorry momma" Uncle Odis started laughing a little and said "I got hurt at work" but it's o.k. "it seem like somebody beat your ass" Boogie" Joanna responded "I mean butt" Odis gave Boogie a hug and said "go back to your room I got to talk to your moma for a second" "O.K." he said then jump down and walk out the kitchen but they knew he was still there but they didn't care Odis said he don't miss a beat do he Joanna said "nope not one" Odis said "You still working", "Yea", it's going good she responded. He said "o.k.", pull out a knot wrap in a rubber band and said This is 2000 get out of the hood, move somewhere like Gwinnett and leave this shit hole behind you o.k. She said "o.k. "I'll start looking today since I'm off. Then he handed her a envelope and said this is for Greg, I'm leaving for a while "Where you going" I don't know yet, just tell him to get with Sam when he get out "He should be getting out in the next 2 years. When he got up headed to the door Boogie ran back a hug him and said "I love you Uncle Odtis" he said "I love you too" take care of ya momma for me "OK Uncle Odis "they watch as Odtis drove off, then Joanna said "Boogie get dress, we going apartment hunting". He ran back to his room and did what he was told.

There was one more stop he had to make, and then he will be gone out of the Dirty south of Atlanta for a long time. He already booked his flight for New York at 1:00 and it was already 11:00 so he didn't have no time to waste. Sam had a source that fuck with Jerry on work all the time and told Sam the layout of Jerry apartment and that usually when he go and cope work. Jerry always to be comfortable with his surrounding meaning he be slipping and would leave the source in the kitchen, go upstairs to get the work so this time when he go upstairs the source gonna unlock the back door for Odis. At first Odis was skeptical but he believes in Sam and his source to come through. When he pulled up to Jerry's apartment his rage and adrenaline started pumping intently he was glad when he pull up there wasn't nobody outside but a couple of junkies that seem more on a mission then he was. He pulled a couple doors down and waited for bout 10 minutes. Sam told him his source was there and just wait until he come out. he knew who it was atomatically when he seen him come out the door. The source look to the right then to the left and smile what Sam told Odis his source will do, to let him know it was done, then walk down the street the opposite way from Odis and was out of sight.

Odis had on all black Dicky suit black air forceies a black "A" fitty cap if anybody was looking, they woulda just guess that he was another dope boy who going to cope work. He had with him a 357 out as he turn the knob it was unlock he went in look around all the light was out then he heard a thump upstairs so he figure Jerry was there, carefully looking in every room down stairs the gun ahead of him at all times he made his way to the stairs, he heard the thump again waited for a second then pursued up the steps, he heard a woman moaning and went in that direction toward the bedroom but made sure he check the other room first, the last room the door was wide open and he seen Jerry doggy styling the Gerry curl bitch he was with at the park, both butt naked and was so into what they was doing they didn't even see Odis standing in the door way. Odis was a O.G. and didn't want to shoot the nigga in the back so he shot in the air, the 357 sounding like a bomb done exploded, shook them out of what they was doing and now both was facing his way. Odis knew he probably done woke or spooked the neighbors but at the moment he didn't care. Jerry started to speak install and said "Odis man what the fuck man I didn't send them boys over there to rob you man". Another shot went off and that hit the women in the chest and she slump over off the bed". Why you do that man", she didn't have nothing to do with it "Don't kill me man" you embarrass me Odis you embarrass me" The next went in Jerry stomach, blood immediately started coming out his mouth, then Odis walk right up to him shoved the gun in his mouth as far as it could go and shot twice, he had one more shot went around the bed where the girl was laying face down put the gun to her head and shot her again to make sure she was dead. He made it to his car and slip out of apartments unseen and unnoticed.

He stop at a nearby gas station to wash his hands and change his clothes he put everything in a garbage bag and the 357 and threw it in the dumpster. He made it to the airport about 12:20 pick up his ticket and went to the pay phone and call Sam. Sam pick up "Hello" Sam this is Odis "I want you to pick up my car in a couple of days and keep it at your house" Odis already hear the noise in the background and knew the house was already bunking with money and eager gamblers ready to drink and gamble it up. "And I will call you when I get to my destination in a couple days" "Alright Odis" "Where you going" Odis said "Don't ask no question, I tell you no lies" I'll keep in touch. Then without another word he hung up. 1:00 flight to New York is now boarding" as he got on the plane sat down he close his eyes and told his self now this always been my dream" as the plane started to take off he relax and felled in a deep sleep.

A person who is hungry or starving will do almost anything to eat.

Even the ones that look like they are making it; usually be the main

Ones that be plotting and be out to get you.

You can always read a person the wrong way and slip up in the hands of a killer a untamed gorilla.

You never know what a person is thinking or what's on a person mind,

"Only God Knows"

Thoughts of Casey Holmes

CHAPTER SEVEN

"Untamed Gorillas . . . .

"Fuck It"

W AS OUR MOTTO AT THE times, we went on our stealing spree,
I met all my friends at the alternative school in Clarkston,
it was a school for kids who got kick out of their regular
school and couldn't go back unless they behavior change. all four of us
was simpler in various ways but, the main thing was we all come from
the projects of Atlanta. Egg was the first person I met he was 12 years old
and was from Grady Homes, a short chubby nigga that kinda remind me
of Humpty Dumpty but was as smoothes with his weight than any fat
kid I ever seen. He always stayed fresh from head to toe because his dad
was a big time dope nigga where he stayed, so he always had fresh gear.
James was 13 year old and was from Carver Homes. He was tall skinny
and black as tare, he was kinda like me, who didn't have no father and
mother who struggle from job to job, he didn't have many good clothes as
Egg but since he was the only child his moma tried to keep him descent.
Meat was 16 years old the oldest out of all of us. He was street tall brown
skin and was from Bruce St some housing project in a small town they
called the L-town. And I was from Denmark, Oakland City, Meat was
the worst off of all of us he didn't have no dad and barley had a mom.
She never came home and when she did never stayed long cause she was
a street walker and was on crack and Meat tell us how he had to lock his
bed room door every time he leave the house cause she always looking
for something to take to the dope man to buy crack. We always meet
up at Avondale train station in the morning, fuck with a couple hoes
try to get them to skip school, then take them to Meat house chill, play

51

Nintendo and smoke weed. Meat had a lot of shit in his room T.V.s like four Nintendos, VCRs, game boys and I used to wonder where he got all of this stuff but I never ask. One day we was all at Meat house done skip school again and Meat said Ya'll wandering where I'm getting all this stuff from aint cha, well I steal it" we all started laughing like meat just told the funniest joke ever but he wasn't laughing so, we stop laughing then he said "yall down" then we look at each other then we all said at the same time "hell yea". "That what got us walking down a side walk in a neighborhood that we knew we didn't belong. Meat stop in front of this big as house "I been peeping this house for a while" aint nobody home, yall down," James said "how you know nobody aint home" I just do so are ya'll coming or what"? Then he already was heading toward the house so we followed. We went to the back door, and meat pulled out a screwdriver the backyard was cover in woods and there wasn't no windows that could be seen from the neighbors. I said "Yo meat I'm having a bad feeling bout this" he said Yo don't worry I got this" then he stuck the screwdriver in the door, it was sliding door but the security bar wasn't attach and couple times stick and bending he finally got the door open, he turn around smile at us and said "come on yall, it should be a lot of nice shit in here" he went in I was right behind him then James and Egg. Egg didn't even get in the door good when we heard yall fucking niggas then a shot rang off. I seen Meat fall but, I thought he just trip everybody was running. I know I ran straight to the woods never look back just ran and ran. I ran for about 2 miles and made it to another neighborhood I didn't know where I was I bent over breathing hard trying to catch my breath then I heard another shot coming from the distance. We told one another if we ever split up we meet back at Avondale train station, I walk out of the neighbor hood I was in and waited at the bus stop and with my luck one was coming up the rode. When I got on the Bus Egg and James was already on there, breathing hard sweating and look like they was scared shitless, I mean I can't lie I was too but, Meat wasn't nowhere in sight. We didn't want nobody to know that we was together so we stayed apart on the bus and just kept staring at one another. The bus pulled over to let bout a dozen police cars with the light blaring and ambulance go by in the direction we just came and we knew it wasn't good, we all knew the ambulance was for Meat, but at the time we was hoping that Meat was gonna show up at Avondale and that ambulance was for somebody else.

The next day at school Egg, James and I made a promise that we wouldn't tell nobody what happen the day before. Soon as we got off the Marta bus the principal said "Joe there somebody in the office that wanna see you and the same thing for you two looking at Egg and James, I walk in the office and there was two detectives both white and old. I told myself "It's over, we caught "The one sitting down said "You Joe right" I nodded my head. Where were you yesterday "I was at home, I was sick" Do you know Travais Roberson" "No" he push a mugshot of Meat in front of me and said "now do you know him" I said "Yea he go to school here" Well he was shot yesterday morning and we was wondering did you see him anytime yesterday" I told you I was at home sick, is he alright". He's dead Joe, he was trying to break in the wrong mans house and got his self kilt" Do you know anything bout that "Joe, Joe, Joe I jump out of the trace just hearing them last couple words "he's dead" Joe!! The detective said "Do you no anything bout that" I told you I was "That you was at home, you told me that "if you hear anything let me know, would you do that". I didn't speak. He gave me a card and said my numbers on there "you can go for now" send your other buddies in would ya pale" I nodded my head saying to myself I'm not your pale pig" I went and sat in a chair between Egg and James, remember the promise both nodded their head. Egg got up and went in next. When Egg came out James went in, them James came out with the principal and the two detectives. The principal said to the detectives yall done with them "Yea we done" The principal said to us" yall boys go to class "we rush off in different directions. We didn't have each other class but we knew we will see each other ather school. It was hard for me to concentrate and probably even harder for Egg and James, cause all I was thinking was about them to words "He dead He's dead He dead it kept running though my mind. I ask to be excused to go to the restroom. Found a empty stall, close the door, sat down on the toilet and broke down in tears.

"Love for Money"

For the love of money, You have to manage it wise

When paper chasing that fetti, You got to be ready to ride

Anyday, any hours, Even when times get tight

You still a money go getta, On all night flight

You ready to fight for it, You ready to brawl

You ready to stunt like ya daddy, You ready to ball

You need to stack that bread, For damage be done

For you be looking at Feds time, Or trying to post bond

I know it seems fun; at the time but, Don't be a dummy

Get what you can out of the game, With love for your money . . . .

By: Casey Holmes

CHAPTER EIGHT

"For The Love of Money"....

THE FUNERAL WAS HELD THE following Saturday at a church in his hood. Since the preacher knew Meat and his mom he knew his moma didn't have no money so he raise some money up to see that Meat had a proper burial. James, Egg and I plan to meet at Indian Creek to catch the 86 Lithonia to attend our friend funeral. We all plan to wear the same thing that day we had on brown dickies slacks, the button down shit, black t shirt ; black all stars and a course the black locs. We got off the bus in front of the hood and people was already walking up to the church since it was right in the middle of the hood didn't nobody drive the only cars you seen was the Hurst to take the body up and around the corner to what they called the hood semetary. As we walk to the door somebody handed us a bishawary then we proceeded to walk down the row to the open casket, Egg and James on the side and me in the middle. The church was pack and the choir was singing, it was so many people in front of us still paying their respect as we made our way closer and closer. When we got in front of the casket we stood there for a moment more of a moment of silence for our friend, then Egg handed me a card and a pen and said "yall sign this fellas" it read:

"To our good friend, the realist nigga we know.
A untamed Gorilla, and a good partner
Rest in peace and may you shine down on us
With much love and much respect.
Love,
The Gorilla Quade

James and I both sign it handed back to Egg, then he put it in the casket with our long lost friend Meat. We found some seats in the back of the church and listen to the preacher, preach and conduct the service, there was so many people there that they had to open the doors and people stood outside listening to the service. Ather the service was over they haul Meat in the husrt and took him to the burial ground we walk there too, but it was right around the corner. There wasn't as many people ther like at the church but, it still was a lot to pay there last respects while they lowered Meat body in the ground.

As we was walking to the bus stop leaving and knew we wasn't ever gonna see this side of town again, somebody behind us said "A fellas hold up for a minute" We stop and stared at the tall man coming our way. He had braids to his shoulder, he had on a Gibo jean outfit and some Trembling boots and when he got closer I seen he had four gold teeth at the top and was husky like he been lifting weights all his life. He said what's up fellas where yall going "I said we finta go we don't know nobody here "He said aint yall from his school "I said yea "He said I know yall don't know me but my name is Bubba but everybody call me bulldog. I said my name Boogie and this here is Egg and James. Bout this time James done lit a blunt and was passing it to Egg. Then Bulldog said Yall boys hungry "Egg said hell yea" Well if yall wanna hang out for a minute and grab something to eat yall more than welcome to come down to the hood, my girl cooking Bar B.Q. I knew Egg was hungry, he always hungry. James said do you mind if we smoke our weed "Bulldog said Hell nall, shit damn near everybody there gonna be smoking yall boys come on down. As we started walking Bulldog said Meat told me a lot about yall" I said he never told us about you. He said Well I was more of a father figure to him and he always talk to me bout what's going on in his life. Egg said he didn't have no Dad. No he didn't Bulldog said but he told me a lot bout yall. Like what I said Well he said that yall was the only friends he had and that yall was loyal to him, he trusted yall a lot. That's where I stay he said as we walk up people was coming out setting up chairs outside, music was playing and the aroma of Bar BQ filled the air, it was a nice day to be outside. A lady with a apron on maybe in her late 40's said Bubba who's ya friends. He introduce us and introduce her as his moma. She said well just call me moma Jay, then ask us was we hungry. Egg said immediately "yes mam" she said" good yall follow me in the house and we can get yall something to eat, drinks I over in that cooler in the corner ova there". While Egg and James follow moma Jay in the house I just went to the cooler found me a chair and sat down. Bulldog said" You aint hungry lil nigga" I said" nall not really maybe later". "That's cool" he said" but, mama Jay gonna make you eat something before you leave", just warning you "I said "that's cool". Nothing was said for a moment, then Bulldog said" Meat was a good dude hum" I said "Yea he was" he said" I told that nigga to slow down doing that shit". I didn't comment, he said "if you and ya boys wanna make some real money halla at me", I said "what you mean" he said "if you and ya homies, wanna make some money just hall at me" I didn't comment. "A look" he said "Meat was selling weed at yall school and was making a lot of money bringing me back my money and still had some left ova for his self". Meat told me yall was good people and I know good people when I see them and them if mama Jay like ya, yall straight with me. Now Egg and James was coming back out the house with plates stack high with food they found they self a chair and sat by me. Egg said "man they got a lot of food in there, mama Jay hook us up too". Bulldog wisper in my ear and said holla at ya boys and get back with me before yall leave" With that he got up and walk away and started conversating with other people at his house.

As we were leaving I talk to Bulldog I said "Yo" we down, what ya got for us "He said That's what up, I'll pick yall up at the train station ather school Monday, yall just be ready to start making serious money" And how that gonna happen anyway" I said I tell yall everything Monday as I turn and walk off he said "Yo Boogie, just have love for the money" I said "My niggas always train to go" As we walk to the bus stop "I was just hoping bulldog wasn't on no bullshit" I told Egg and James we be meeting with him ather school, they agreed. As we wait on the bus to go home we talked bout Meat and the good times we had being the "Gorilla Quade" but on and off we was thinking about the money we was finta make, james fired up another blunt.

In the hood kids grow up fast not because they want too because they have too;

Just to survive in the territory of their community. They live how they see

Everybody else live and the only way they can support their selves or their family is to

Do what everybody else does

You wouldn't understand if you wasn't from the hood so, don't perpetrate or

Discriminate a person' especially if you not trying to help or make their lives better.

Don't knock the hustle because in the hood it's "Survivor of the fittest," that just

How it is where I'm from . . . .

Thoughts of Casey Holmes

I don't know, which way to go

Should I go fast, or should I go slow

Should I walk, or should I run

Will I be carrying a knife, or carrying a gun

If I make it, To see another day

Will I go, or will I stay

Will I stand, or will I lay

Will ti be short distance, or far away

"I just don't know"

By: Casey Holmes

"Grady Baby Train"

In dusty heat, treacherous snow and thunderous rain,

Staying down in the dirty south, Is part of our thing,

We are known for our swag, We are known for our slang

We was born in the heart of Atlanta, Raised up grady babies train . . . .

By: Casey Holmes

CHAPTER NINE

Grady Baby Train . . . .

A THER SCHOOL MONDAY, BULLDOG WAS waiting for us at the train station just like he said he would. We walk toward his, he was driving a clean blue 72 Cutless with the cutless ralleys and the blue leather seats. I got in the front James and Egg in the back. As we rode off James said "Yo Dog" can I fire up this blunt "Long as you don't burn my seats nigga he said "Didn't nobody say nothing for awhile we just sat smoking waiting for Dog to tell us what we was gonna do. We pull up to his crib he said yall hungry "Egg said hell yea I said nigga you always hungry "Dog said Mama Jay cooking something now it should be done in a minute. James said you got any blunts dog said yea. We walk in you can smell Mama Jay cooking something a humming a song to herself Egg walk straight for the kitchen and James behind him. Dog said you gonna eat I said knall he said damn Boogie you don't never eat I said cause I'm hungry for some money with a little smirk on my face he said that's what's up, but don't starve yourself, knall I'm straight I said. When Egg came out he had neck bones, rice and cornbread, James just had a drink in his hand Egg said man mamma Jay know she be hooking it up. Dog said yea she can make a nigga feel at home. James said Yo Dog what's up with a blunt. I got ya my nig, let go upstairs. When we got to Dog room it was a big box look like just came from UPS, I glance at the label it said Maryland but that's all I seen. He said the last one close the door. He went to the closet pulled out a scale and big sandwich bags and said yall take a seat. He ran back down the steps came back up with a plate to and started eating. He pointed to me and said start opening that box I said what this box he said yea so I did. It was a big square wrap in thorough form wrap so tight that you couldn't see what was wrap inside. I was like what is this he said you see, hold tight. He got finish eating grab a box cutter and started tearing into the form when he got finish he rip it open the smell was out of this world. I wonder if the whole neighbor hood smelt it but the size of a big square block of weed was breath taking he pulled a little off hand it to James and said the blunts is over there rolled that shit up and tell me what you think. James said hell yea I will. Dog said we got to get this shit bag up fast so hurry up. He said everything on 57.8 in one of these bags. I stood there still overcome by how much weed was in front of me Dog said hurry up nigga, I jump out of my trance and started pulling and weight and bagging up the weed. When we got done there was 50 pound of weed stack up neatly in the corner. He gave all of us 4 onces and said I want 200 from all yall, I said how long do we got "he said the quicker yall come back the more you'll get. As we was leaving Dog pull me to the side and said yo watch ya boy for me I said who he said James, he smoke a lot and I don't want him to fuck up his money, Egg seems like he will do good but, I don't know bout James I said he be ok but I keep a eye on him though. That's whats up, just make sure, I said that's whats up. He drop us off at the train station and said a fellas don't get hight off ya on supply that's the number one rule with that he drove off. Egg said how yall planning on getting yall share off I said I might give mines to my brother. I don't know, what about you, well I can always get some of my dads client tell cause he been trying to get me to serve a couple people for him when he's away any. Egg said we both look at James and I said what bout you he was already in the mist of rolling a blunt he said I don't know yet but as I think about it, lets smoke I was thinking I hope James don't smoke all his profit up but I think he will be ok.

When I got home, I quickly made it to my room close the door and lock it I think my momma was home but sleep but still didn't want her to walk in on me. I layed everything out on the bed and I got 4 onces what the fuck um gonna do with 4 ounces. I thought of my brother Brandon then shooked off telling myself he might just take it from me and not give me shit. Then I thought about telling Uncle Odis and remember he was out of town, then it hit me Sam Uncle Odis right hand man. I would skip school tomorrow and halla at Sam, yea I'll go over Uncle Odis house where Sam probably be and ask Sam, yea that's what I'll do. I put the weed up just in time my momma tried to walk in seeing that the door was lock she said "boy why this door lock", I said I didn't know it was lock", she said" what you doing? I said nothing "she said", how was school, I said "fine" she said" well take a bath and get ready for tomorrow" I said "ok". I said "mama you ok she said yea just tired", I'm going back to sleep babe just have a good day ok. I said "ok". Then she handed me 5 dollars and said that should be anuoff right I said "yes mam I'll be ok", with a worry look in her eyes she said "you been going to school haven't ya" I said" yes mama", knowing I wasn't planning on going tomorrow, she said "ok", I don't want them people to call me and tell m e you aint bee going, I was thinking to myself if them people call you, you probably want know anyway but, I said yes mama. She left close my door back. I kick off my shoes just staring at the ceiling thinking about the weed and what tomorrow may bring, then drifted off to sleep.

I woke up early the next morning to take a quick bath and change clothiers grab my stash and walk out the door to the bus stop. I knew Egg and James would be waiting for me to show up at the train station but today they would miss me cause I was on a paperchace a (term) I heard my brother say before and it sounded real good with what I was up to at the moment and I smile at myself cause I wanted some money and all I had left was 3.75 cause of the bus fair so I headed toward Uncle Odis house. I got off the bus and it was people already walking around with beer bottles and half sleep looking like zombies. I didn't stare I just walk straight to Uncle Odis house cause I didn't want nobody asking me no question or maybe try to take my shit so I hurried. I made it to the house and was finto knock on the door when this guy emerge out of nowhere, wearing dirty cloths, ashy as hell even his hair was dirty and as he got closer he even smelled bad. He had a 24 oz can of Blue Bull in his hand and just for a moment I thought about Greg. Then the guy said "what you doing over here", where you going". I felt like a cat had my tongue for a moment then I said nuna ya business. He said everything my business then the house door open and it was Sam. He was shocked at the moment then he said Boogie I ran up to the door. He said what ya doing here boy, you know ya Uncle aint here right I said yea, but I need to talk to you, he pulled me inside, look at the guy who was out front and said nigga, didn't I tell you stop hanging around here this time of day. The guy said my bad Sam Um gone Sam close the door. I was glad not to see nobody there at the time. Then Sam ask what you need to see me for? Don't you pose to be in school lil nigga I said yea but I got something to show you, what you got nigga? Man if ya mama knew you was here she'll kill me.

I pulled the weed. He said boy where you get this from, you robbing people now nigga? It was more of a answer then a question but I said na'll Sam, somebody gave it to me to sell he look at me in my eyes and knew I wasn't lying. Then he said so what you want me to do? Sell it if you can. He study the 4 ounces for a moment then said How much do you want? I didn't know I just knew Dog wanted 200 hundred back so I said what you give me for it he said Boogie since it's you I'll give you 400 he reach in his pocket and gave me 400 dollar bills. He said can you get some more I said yea he said well bring me 4 more tomorrow and I'll get that from you too. I said thanks Sam as I was walking out the door he said you need to take ya ass to school but was smiling when he said this and close the door. All I was thinking is that I just sold all of it in one day made Dog his money and made me $200 I caught the bus still smiling knowing I was going back to Dog house right then.

I walk up to Dog door and knock it only took him a minute to open the door. He said what's up Boogie what ya doing here and where ya homies, I said, I need to talk to you, he let me come in. He said what's up. I gave him his money and another hundred cause i wanted to keep a hundred for myself he said Damn nigga you already done with that shit with a smile on his face i said yea can you do something else for me. he said I got ya he pulled out another bag this had 6 ounces he said sinec you gave me a hundred I'm throwing in 2 eacha so you still owe me 200$ thats cool lil nigga i said yea thanks. He said Boogie you smoking i said I ain't got nothing to smoke with that he gave me like a 20 sack and said that's good you remember what i said, Yea don't get high off ya own supply i said he said Good good you learning. As i was leaving he said stay down lil nigga i nodded while twisting me up a blunt, fired it up and walk to the bus stop.

I didn't make to school that whole week cause every time i went to Sam he bought everything from me in double and i go right back to Dog give him his money and he front me more and more. I didn't know how Egg or James was doing and act the moment i didn't care, I was getting money that I was sitting on about a 1000$ about 10 ounces, that Sam was getting from me tomorrow, and just owed Dog 500$ I was thinking about just paying Dog the whole grand but I didn't want him to think that I was getting money like that, I told him about Sam and everything but, he know he was just buying whatever I cop from him and I bring him his money then he front me some more but, I never told him how much I was putting up Sam told me never let your right hand know what the left hand is doing, he said "don't trust nobody" and then on I didn't, hell i didn't even trust myself with this shit, all i knew that I was getting to the money and wanted more.

"Living That Life"

We live that life of. dreams and fantasies

Some people still believe, Money grow on trees

The quicker it comes, The quicker it goes

Really doesn't matter if you got it, You still can turn broke

With a flicker of the eye, It will all be gone

You must done lost your mine, All that money you blown

Now you are remanicing, On the thing you had

You want never have it again, If you dwell on the past of living that life . . . .

By: Casey Holmes

CHAPTER TEN

Living That Life . . . .

I T BEEN 4 YEARS AND I stop hanging around Egg and James for awhile not because I wanted to but because I was get money and felt like I could handle myself. The last time I seen them was the day I drop out of school. I mean "I found out at 18 I could go and get my own papers so that what I did. Dog still inform me on how they was making out he say Egg he was doing good and was coping more onces but was mainly coping cloth". You know how he likes to stay fresh" I said yea that's Egg for you. And James he said James paid him back a couple time but other that he started just tell him he had to buy his own, That when I noticed that he wasn't saving any money he said he just start buy 2 onces at a time then one, so I knew then he was smoking more than he was selling "I said I tried to slow that nigga down on the smoking shit, but you can't tell nobody nothing. You right lil nigga, so what going on with ya? The same thing I said, by then I was coping ponds for a 1,00 and Sam was paying 12, so I was making a 200 profit. I didn't mind cause if it wasn't for Sam I wouldn't have shit. Greg still haven't got out come to find out he was doing feds time so he had to do day for day, so since I didn't have no father didn't know where my brother was, I look up to Dog for guides, I went from weed to coke in no time and I even started snorting the shit. I didn't see nothing wrong the first couple times I start doing it but then it just got worse and worse, I just got addicted to it. My money I save started getting low and I started losing a lot of weight. Staying up all times a night, then stop even going home. I knew I was doing bad when I started to see my money decrease, even though I was still making a little here and there, but more and more it went up my nose. I started looking bombie and wearing the same clothiers all week long, really trying to stay down on my paper cache but slowly and slowly going under. I even stop fuckin with Sam cause I didn't want him to know, so my money was getting shorter and shorter and my time was being more wasted doing coke every day, staying up all night and wishing the shit would get better. Dog was serving off my coke habit and seems to not care if I was falling off or not, long ass he got his money, so I was lost, confuse but refuse to give up. I thought I was just living that life of what I seen Greg, Odis, Sam, Egg, James and Dog and my brother living, but it seems like living that life of a street nigga had more consequences than I imagine, I guess it was more I had to learn, but at the moment I was alone and even though I knew nobody wasn't gonna fuck with me, I was even scared at times, but I never led on to nobody and was destine to keep my head up. Thinking to myself "Damn I hate this shit" as I noted up another line of coke.

The streets can turn a person into a monster and that monster can turn

a person insane, but we can't never give up trying to accomplish to

succeed in our goals and what God have in stored for us. All we can do is
believe, keep the faith

change the way we think and live better . . . .

Thoughts of Casey Holmes

CHAPTER ELEVEN

Dead Cracker Head . . . .

S OME HOW WORD GOT OUT that I was doing bad and was fucking up big time in the L-town. I was standing outside in the trap not doing nothing but wanna know how I can come up to get me something to snot, but since I was broke I didn't even have no money to eat, not that I wanted to eat, I was just hungry cause I wanted something to snot instead of food now that's bad.

A car pulled up right in front of me, it was burgany Chevy camprice brohem with some 20in crom flats and limo tint. As I was finto walk off someone had jump out of the passenger side and said "Boogie" I turn around to see my brother Brandon. I didn't know how to respond I was stuck, but I didn't have to say nothing he said come on man, we finto go "I didn't say nothing he said you straight I said yea, feeling more embarrass then anything by letting him see me like this, then the fear of him knowing that I was using cocaine. I just jump in the back seat. Who was driving Red, but he didn't say nothing probably out of the respect for my brother, but I bet he was thinking "damn this nigga look like a junky, but in my mind I felt the same way. All Brandon said was "you going with me" Red turn up the music and I sat back close my eyes and was grateful to have a brother who love me enough to take me away from the one place I didn't want to be anymore and was thankful to be save.

Doing the drive neither one of us spoke a word to each other I don't know if Brandon felt bad by seeing his little brother like he was or he was trying to figure out what he was going to do. When we road pass our exit on I-20 I was kind of relieve to know he wasn't taking me to see moma cause I woulda been a shame to let her see me like this and maybe he would have too, but he still never said anything until we jump on 285 going towards Greenbria. You know ya cousin down here I said who like I really cared but I was glad he was talking to me. Your cousin Rollin. Oh for real I said he said yea, we going over there now. I wanted to ask why, but I never did just sat back and wasn't another word spoke. When we road pass Greenbria I was thinking do cuz stay in College Park, but I got my answer when rode pass Camp creek and got off at Washington Rd. we pulled in a apartments called Candlewood, To myself I was like damn these some nice apartments the we stop. Brandon said get out for a minute. I was relunate for a minute cause I didn't want to see nobody and definitely didn't want nobody to see me, but I got out. We walk down some stairs. Brandon said this where ya cousin stay "The door open and a tall light skin ballhead nigga was standing there. I knew who he was off the rip he said what's up cousins. We hug and his greeting was warm and comforting and I was glad to be there at the moment I haven't seen him in a long time. He was fresh from head to toe, he had on a light blue Nike jump suite with the light blue Nike air max but to top everything off h e had a big ass gold rope with a grenade piece hanging from it, To myself I was like man this nigga know he's fresh.

I sat down on the couch Rollin and Brandon went in the kitchen to have a conversation, I hope it wasn't bout me. Brandon came back out, he look at me and said come here, we walk down the hall to a bedroom; he said yo this is my room, but I don't be here much so you can stay here. I said preciate cha. He said I know what been going on witcha and I'm sorry I wasn't in ya life, you are my lil bro and um gonna get ya right ya hear me. I said yea with tears filling my eyes I manage to hold them in, but it seems like the feeling was mutual cause I kind seen Brandon eyes water up a little, but we knew both was trying to be tuff. He said You look tired. I said I am, he said well go ahead and go to sleep and I'll be back tomorrow to come get you. All I could say was thank you he said don't worry about it I love you Boogie. I said I love you too then he left. I was so tired so I jump in the bed, falling asleep thinking about how can I help my brother get right, whatever he needs me to do, I'm gonna do it I don't care if it kills me. My mind was back on the grind and all I could see was them Dead crackerheads.

Some people grew up with loving personality that would not ever

Change for no one, even if someone do you wrong; it just seems like

Your love always just take over the harden of your heart.

You could always have more than one mentor with different opinions . . . .

Thoughts of Casey Holmes

CHAPTER TWELVE

Passion For Love

BEFORE I DROP OUT OF school and my brother came to the rescue of destroying my life. I met Pookie. It was a hot raining summer, I met her from a friend who had a friend. That day I rode the bus to Hambrick Rd. I didn't know what to expect, it was more like a blind date. I knock on the door. Who is it? my mind was racing and didn't hear the question the first time. Who is it? the voice said the second time, it's Joe I said with a couple of locks the door came open. I walk in I seen a beauty. She was 5.8 like 185, brown eyes, short hair and a ass out of this world. I you could literally put a glass of water on her ass and it would of not falling. She didn't have no gut that you would of thought probably would of been there, but she was just thick, no gut and a big ass. I was 18, young, dumb and full of cum and seeing that ass, my dick immediately rose. She said you hungry I said a little bit, but I didn't know if my hunger was for her of if I really had an appetite so I said I straight right now. she said well come on up. We walk up some stair, still in a daze walking behind her thinking damn shorty fine. We sat on the bed and since she already had on a night gown. I said can I get a little bit more comfortable she said go ahead as I was taking my shoes off my clothes just kinda disappeared like magic and I was under the cover with her, kissing on her neck, I was thinking damn it feel so hot between her thighs and I wanted to be in them. I made my way from her neck to her nipples oh they was big but fits her whole body for me. I started massaging her tities with my tongue and one hand while the other hand was playing with the inside of her thighs oh she was wet and hot and I just wanted so bad to be inside her. I jump in between her legs now hunching the inside of this hot and wet pussy. She moan I kiss her plump juicy soft

85

lips my dick was already hanging outside of my boxer from the slot so I move her pantie to the side. Inside this fat wet and hot pussy I went. The exacy was like nothing else her pussy was like a heater. I lift her legs grab her ass chick spread them open in the air and drove myself deeper inside. She was coming all on my dick while moving her ass in the air, like I really thought she look like a belly dancer. Her pussy got hotter and I feel myself ready to explode but the passion that I was feeling made me stay in a little longer. I couldn't think my mind was so full of this sexy ass lady who giving me something I never had and it was feeling good. I started stroking harder and harder to I just couldn't hold it anymore I came and we both sat there daze. I never had a woman and didn't know what was coming next, but I know I wanted to explore her body again. I didn't care, all I knew that I just wanted to make more love with her and I didn't ever want it to stop. I guess that what you call passion for love because at the time it felt like both. And every time it goes more intense and better. That was my first experience of passion for love.

"Greedy Green"

See you walk and talk, with the ambition of none

With the neither fear of nor man, while carrying your gun

Arriving on the scene, with the point of profit

Eliminating a lot of things, so your mind in mountains

Rivers, springs, valleys, oceans and hills

Your mind is on your family, so anybody you kill

See you always been a hustler, so your mind aint like that

Army fatigue, jumping out of trees, so now your mind is combat

Maybe just come back up, forgetting yourself in that bind

You staying down regardless, even if the price of you is dying

I understand if the price, is your family in need

All you have to do is, get right and maintain with your greedy in greed

By: Casey Holmes

CHAPTER THIRTEEN

Greedy Green

I WOKE UP THE NEXT EVENING with a slight knock at the bedroom door, it was my cousin Rollin, he said You gonna sleep all day, I said what time is it he said 1:00 gone head and get up and come talk to me, I'll be in the living room, I said aight, then he close the door back. It took me a second to get my mind right, but eventually I got up, put back on my clothes and shoes and walk up front to the living room. Rollin said ya hungry "I said a little bit, well there some cereal in there so I walk to the kitchen seen a box of fosted flacks, got me a bowl poured me some cereal grab a spoon and was already munching before I left the kitchen. What up cousin Rollin said What up my nig, What you been up too? Rollin ask nothing just chilling I said "Well Brandon called and said he'll be back probably later on tonight. I said that's what's up. A knock came at the door and Rollin got up to answer it, but out of nowhere he produce a tec 9 in his hand I didn't say nothing but Rollin look back at me like I pose to be surprise, I mean why would I be, I been around hustlers and killers all my life, I just stared at the door. He open it and two dudes come in. they seen me said what's up but I didn't respond. I was thinking to myself first of all I don't know you second of all you don't know me but I was raise to stay alert and whatch everything around me. Don't trust nobody and stay out of other people business. When Rollin close the door I put down my bowl cause if this nigga have to carry a gun to open his door I want to be on point too. Rollin told the dudes to hold on for a minute and he went to the back I was wondering what the fuck this nigga up to. The two dudes look at me then stared at the TV. The first one said shit what you watching. I didn't say nothing so I guess he took as this nigga aint gonna say nothing to us, but he is watching us. And I was thinking to myself you damn right nigga. I been on the streets to long and I knew shady sneaky motherfucker when I see them and these dudes wasn't right. the second dude was looking kind of jittery and was turning his head back and forth to the door to his homeboy to me and I seen in his eyes that I wasn't suppose to be here right now. well motherfucker I am "I thought, but what was going on. I walk to the door made sure it was lock then to the kitchen to put the bowl up, but kept my eye on these creepy ass nigga in the living room. "What the fuck was cuzzo doing back there so long "I thought, now looking in the kitchen draws for a knife or something, as I rumble looking for something useful, I hear a slight thub at the door, I mean it coulda been anything, the wind a acorn any kind of debreen flying around out there. I found a crome 380 thanks goodness that my cuzing keep a tool in the kitchen. I checked to see was it loaded it was, now I feeling better. The second dude went to the door and was finta unlock it or maybe leave or something I don't know and I didn't care with the 380 in my hand, I said what the fuck ou doing? He turn around and said I'm just going to the car for a second. I said "fuck that nigga you don't never open that door nigga, we don't play that shit you hold the fuck up" Rollin finally came back up and said "yo cuzin what's going on? "I said these nigga trying to open ya door my nig and I'm not going fa that shit "the first dude said Rollin man tell ya cousin to chill out" I said fuck you nigga, you don't know me homeboy "And while you talking nigga tell your homeboy to lock that door back "pointing the 380 at the door. What the fuck going on? Rollin ask me, but I didn't respond and never took my eyes off these dudes who was standing there. The first dude said "man ya peoples tripping and turn around and headed for the door. I said "didn't I just tell ya'll nigga don't open that door mutherfucker "it was too late the door flew open and two mask men rush in one with a 9mm and the other look like he had a 38 revolver. All I heard was "yall lay down" The two dudes fell on the floor off the rip, but the mask men seems like they didn't see them. Soon as the mask men walk over the thresh hold Rollin started bustin, I started bustin the two mask men started bustin. Rollin open up the first nigga chest with the tec 9, he didn't have a chance. The one with the 38 seen his partner fall so he was backing out the door, but the second dude who was laying on the floor jump up and ran behind the dude and push him back in the door trying to get out, but I caught that nigga in the leg he fell outside the door. I seen him trying to crawl away, the dude with the 380 ran out of bullets he drop the gun and put his hands up saying Please don't shoot me, I ran up to him and put a bullet right in his head. On the way out the door to catch up with the other motherfucker who I shot in the leg I didn't have to go far cause he was still right outside trying to drag his self away. I said "where the fuck you think you going" kick him in the face made him turn over, then shot him two time in the chest. I ran back in the door and Rollin was over the other one who was on the floor with the tec in the back of his head. Rollin said Cuzzo I didn't respond I just stood there staring down at that nigga on the floor with so much anger, tears ran down my cheeks and a smoky gun in my hand. Rollin said cuzzo "I walk right up to the dude on the floor put the 380 to his head and pulled the trigger, nothing happen I pulled again and again and again unitl Rollin had to get the gun out of my hand and said cuzzo cuzzo I finally look at Rollin in his eyes he said grab that bag I drop I look back at the dude on the floor and started kicking him in the head You peise of shit". You dumb motherfucker, "I told yall, I told yall I told ya, this shit aint no hoe, I told yall motherfucker, then Rollin shot him, still kicking the nigga in the head even though he was dead, Rollin said yo cousin, yo cuzzo still kickin yo Boogie then he grab me by the shoulders and pulled me back, he said "look at me" I did he said they are dead my nig, they are dead, he said a cuz you got to go ok. I said cuz I'm not leaving you, he said everything gonna be straight just go, "I'm gonna tell Brandon to pick you up at the store, take this he handed me a big black garbage bag and said go out the back door, it's a trail that lead you straight to the store "go nigga now" I kick the nigga again he said "go now the police on the way, "go nigga!! So I ran out the back door. I turn around just say "Rollin I love you my nig, he said I know now go nigga!!

I found the trail and made it to the store but I stayed duck off in the woods looking at the traffic of people standing outside looking at the police cars that race up Washiton Rd headed toward where I just came from. Fuck Fuck I'm cursing myself for leaving I didn't want to leave my cuz up there alone, but knew he was right, I didn't know how he was gonna get hisself out of this shit, but he must knew what he was talking about. Breathing hard and sweating like a camel with no warter cursing myself. I done seen almost a dozen police cars already and it look like a dozen more headed the same way. What time is it I thought, I remember when Rollin told me it was 1:00 oclock so it mus be 2 or 3 by now. I can't believe these niggaz tried to rob my people and they did that shit during the day. What the fuck wrong with motherfucker. Still furious and tired from running I finally seen Red and my brother pulled up to the plaza, more police going up. Brandon, go out looking around looking for me then walk in the store. Feeling that the close is clear. I emerge from the woods with the bag over my shoulder and walk straight to the car and got in the back "thank God Red got this limo tint" My brother came back out the store and jump in, turn around look at me said "ya aight" I said "yea" He look at Red and said "lets ride". When we got on 285 I started breathing a little better. Brandon handed me a blunt and the weed made me feel better it ease the tension and the addrilling that I had and I felt better, but still thinking about what just happen as we rode away from East point in silence.

"Hard Times"

Hard times have us going through, So many dramatic situation

Running from parole probation, Giving us chances of catching more cases

Cause it hard living a life of, Violence and disasters

A beast with no master; a smile with no laughter, And a pull pit with no pastor

See it's hard for thy people. To comprehend and understand

That we have to grow up and stand, And life is base on a destinynated chance

So we go through life in the thoughts of, Going coming living it

Society got our minds thinking our skin is, infected convicted with sentences

So it hard for us to figure out or understand, what the world stores or really about

Our minds are stuck on the streets, and the revolving doors closing with no way of getting it out

The world got us thinking that, we are nobody we are nothing

That is why most of us surviving and bucking, and half of us are still broke and struggling

Cause we don't know which way to go, should we go fast should we go slow

Our minds be so infected with addictive drugs, that we just don't know

So if we don't find that right knowledge, or walk down that positive straight line

We will always be and forever be, in the aspects of hard times . . . .

By: Casey Holmes

CHAPTER FOURTEEN

"Hard Times"

W E CHECK INTO A RED Roof Inn, just in time to see the breaking news on Fox 5, we watch in silence as the white reporter told us the story.

"This is Rosie Oconner reporting in East Point apartment complex called The CandleWood. They say a man name Rollin Jenkins have shot and kill four arm men who apparently tried to rob him. They say three of the men did have guns in their possession and two of the men was wearing ski mask. The police say that Mr. Jenkins did have a tec 9 simi automatic that was indeed registering in his name and are still investigating the case and couldn't give me no more information at this time, but they are looking at this as a home invasion, but the case is currently under investigation at the moment."

John reporter: Did they say what the motive might have been for as drugs or anything like that?

D Conner: Well John, they did say that it was not no drugs in the house, but Mr. Jenkins was wearing a lot of expensive jewelry that might cause these men to try to rob him, but they still looking into all the fact at this time and trying to find out more from Mr. Jenkins at this time.

John: Did they take Mr. Jenkins down to the Police station or is he still there as we speak.

O'Conner: No John, they did indeed take Mr. Jenkins down to the police station to question him more but one officer did tell me that Mr. Jenkins is charge with multiple homicides and will be currently awaiting trial on these charges.

John: Thank you Rosie for this brief summary on this late breaking story.

O'Conner: You welcome John, this is Rosie O'Conner with the late breaking story and we will keep you inform, with more to come, this is Rosie O'Conner signing off.

John: We should have more information on this story on Fox 5 news a ten. Now to the weather.

We turn the TV down and we all sat there for a moment passing a blunt around. Brandon said man what happen? I told them what happen and how I felt a bad vibe with these dudes. I said "though what got me is how the police said there wasn't any drugs in the house". I answer my own question, when I thought of the trash bag Rollin gave me. Then we all look down at the same time at the trash bag in the corner. I got up and grab the bag and poured everything out on the bed. There was 30 pounds of weed indiversavly bag, a scale and the 380 I use. I told them about the gun. Brandon said "we just have to destroy that I said but what we gonna do with all this weed "Like I didn't know the answer. Well we need to get it off and wait for them people to give cuz a bond "Brandon said I said "that's what's up" Red said "Fa show" Brandon said y'all know cuz bond gonna be sky high, so we gonna have to grind all this and maybe have to flip this shit more than once, so right now let's get this money fashaw cuz "Fashaw cuz" we all said and sat there to finish the blunt.

So what do we suppose to do about this time of virtue?

All we can do is; stand tall, gain structure and be all you

Can be; is what we called "war war 3 on the streets"

The bottom line is; if you gonna struggle, get money or

Just continue to struggle, to be broke. So what you

Gonna do? Bar B.Q. or mildew? It's all on you.

<Atlanta is the stumping ground>Georgia is the battlefield> . . . .

Thoughts of Casey Holmes

CHAPTER FIFTEEN

"Street Soldier" . . . .

A s WE SET OFF ON our way to grind this weed and get this money, since Rollin gave it to me, my brother was respectful to me even though he was older he still ask me for my opinion. Well, I said You and Red take 20 and I'll handle 10. Brandon said what you gonna do? I said shit get on the grind he said you sure, you ok? I knew he was just concern bout me, so I didn't get upset. I just said Just give me a couple days I'll be straight while looking at him dead in the eye's, he knew that I wasn't playing and he knew then he could trust me to do what I said he said aight then little bro. so what you finto do now? I said well my nig, I'm finto jump in the shower then I'm heading out. He said where you going? I said I'm straight my nig, just let me get bout ten bucks to catch the bus. He gave me twenty and said well, me and Red finto go, but we got this room all night, so if you need somewhere to stay huh hear go one of the keys to the room, he handed me the key. He said I probably be back later, but if not "man" just be careful o.k. lil bro, I said "O.K. my nig", as they walk toward the door I said Yo B, you be careful too aight luv ya, he said aight love you too my nig. I started toward the shower, turn the water on went back to sit down for a minute to think about what in the hell um gonna do with this weed, but it didn't take me long to know, first name that pop up was Sam.

I took a shower, got dress, jump on the bus and headed to see Sam. I left everything behind and secured it as best as I could in the room, I didn't want to take nothing with me on this trup cause first of all I didn't even know if Sam would fuck with me and secondly I didn't know if he was there, so I decided to leave everything and just in case the maids haven't clean up yet, I put the do not disturb sign on the outside of the door.

I made it to the hood, jump off the bus and as usual the Gambling house was jumping hard and it seems like the streets never sleep cause people was out and about doing what they do best, whatever that may be. I knock on the door anticipating on what to say. I had to knock and second time much harder cause the music was blasting Al Green "With last two dollars", I not gonna lose, these last two dollars, I'm not gonna lose, one for the bus fair, the other for the junk box to give me the blues" The song made me think, how many people done really lost their last two dollars, gamble it up because they just didn't know when to get up and leave? The thought left my mind instantly when the door open. It was Sam, he was turn around telling somebody to change the cassette, when he turn around and look at me. He said Boogie!! I said what's up Sam, we just look at each other for one quick hot second, I couldn't tell if he was mad at me or just looking at me cause I was so thin, but a big grin came across he face and he gave me a hug and walk me in the house, pass everybody and to the backroom and close the door. We sat down, then he said I'm glad to see you, you know ya uncle Odtis been asking about you? I was finta ask was he here, but Sam read my mind put up his hand up and said He's not here, and I didn't tell him nothing, what been going on with you, I didn't say nothing. He left the room and came back with a Budweiser, close the door again, (people was laughing having a good time in the background) Sam said "ya know I'm not stupid right? I know what you been doing, you know we O.G.s know everything that goes on, on the streets. I didn't speak he said "I sent ya brother out there to get ya, when ya stop coming arould I knew something was wrong, then I heard from a source that you was fucking up out there bad, look you don't have to explain nothing to me, you still my nigga aight now com give me a hug." I did, and then sat back down. "I seen what happen over at ya cousin house" he continues "man" that's fuck up" I even heard you fuck up a couple them suckers, "but he said this with a grin. "What I told you I know everything "I just stared at him, he said did they give him a bond yet" I said we still waiting for them too. He nodded his head in understanding. I said "we trying to get his bond money up that why I'm here to talk to you about. He said "how much you got". I said "well we sell what we got he said "nigga" didn't I tell ya I know everything "Boogie", so how many you got "I said 10 pounds" he said I want all of them tomorrow aight, I said ok he said try to get here early ok I said I'll be here. He said "the same price right I said yea" he said if you need me you know I'm here fa ya I said thanks Sam, got up walk to the door and said I'll see you tomorrow. He said aight. The bus just pulled up right on time, Sam said behind me "be safe boy" I got on the bus headed back to the room to get things ready for the next day.

CHAPTER SIXTEEN

"Big Face C-Notes".....

They say "money is the root of all evil", but society can't live or survive without making some kind of income. That's why there is precisely a million and one ways to get money that means; there is more than a million. Half of the ways are right and half are wrong; so if you ask me how; I would choose to get my <Big Face C-Notes> I probably would say "By any means necessary" . . . .

Thoughts of Casey Holmes

WHEN I GOT BACK TO the room, everything was just how I left it. I walk to the store and purchase two cheap duffle bags one bigger than the other cause I was planning on putting everything in the small one and the big over that one for it what the weed want be to smelling when I make the trip back. I got some car freshener to spray on the weed to keep some of the smell down and a blunt to smoke. Brandon and Red was there when I got back from the store, they was talking and counting money. They look up at me and Brandon said "what's up my nig" I said chilling "Brandon said" you had any process with that "I said" I'll have the money in the morning "Brandon and Red look at each other I knew they was thinking how this nigga gonna sell all that shit by the morning, but Brandon just said "That's wuz up" he said "me and Red we got off ten already I said "cool" not wanting to know all their business. I went to retrieve my stash and stuff it in the duffel bag then over lap it with the other and started to spray the freshener over the weed, I knew they was looking at me, but didn't say nothing. When I got done, I put the bag in the corner, I knew I would have to spray it again in the morning before I leave but it seems that everything will go ok with how I had it, so I was please.

I walk over to one of the chairs in the corner where the table was, since Brandon and Red was using the bed, I sat down in the chair prop my legs up and to rest my eyes, but never fallen asleep cause I was so thinking bout the money tomorrow. Brandon said we got the room for another day so we straight tomorrow too. I said "fashow" Red said "I got somebody that want 2 of them things now, so we got to go. They cleared off the bed and headed toward the door, I said "Yo bra" I'll have the

113

money tomorrow, so we gonna need some more aight "Aight he said" I'll see you tomorrow then". I was glad to see them leave, not because I didn't enjoy my brother company cause I just wanted to lay down. I got up, took my shoes off and laid across the bed and went to sleep.

I got up early bout 6:00 to see Brandon laying on the bed and Red in the chair. I woke Red up and told him he can lay on the bed, he said aight lil bro, he seem me getting ready to leave and said "you need a ride" I said na'll my nig um straight, just tell Brandon I'll be back bout 1:00 he said "that's what's up" then laid down and went back to whatever dream he was having. I sprayed the weed and the bag some more with the freshener, walk out the room and jump on the bus. At first I was paranoid as hell cause the bus was pack with early morning people going to work, but then it was good too, that it was crowded cause didn't nobody pay me any mind, so I come down a little and got myself more comfortable for the ride.

I was so paranoid when I got off the bus and headed toward the trains and until I got on the train. I knew I didn't have nothing to worry about cause Marta was so congested with the early morning crowdness I knew I was ok, maybe it was that I never carried so much before with me. I felt like all eyes were on me. Aight Boogie remain calm don't look suspicious just remain calm everything gonna be ok. I kept tell myself. I knew this was the best time to transfer a load like this but you still have to be aware of everybody, even though it was pack and every seat was took. I was like standing in the door way of the train, just in case I have to get off quick, believe me if that happens, I was determine to take my bag with me. Five Points is your next station the intercom buzz and took me out of my thought. I knew I had to transfer from the East bound to South Bound, but that shouldn't be no problem, long as I don't have to leave the train station, I'll be straight. I just know Five points is where they keep most of the police. The door came open, I walk with the crowd I knew it should still be a crowd on the south bound and was relieved when it was. I settle back at a far end waiting for the train. I was so happy it didn't take long to come. This train was pack and had more luggage cause majority of the people was probably going to the airport. I had a couple more stops then I'll be home free. West-End is your next stip they announce over the intercom. The train slowed and stop, the door came open I step out, but out of now where two Marta police emerge from the train too and started walking in my direction. One was talking to his walky talky on his shoulder still walking towards me. I made it almost to the stairs when they started running moving people out the way. It was so crowded I didn't want to push nobody down the stairs, so I just waited as calm as I could, when they made it up to where I was I almost shitted on myself. I didn't breath, I knew it was over, but they ran right pass me and went down the stairs steadily moving people out the way. I didn't breathed or move it seems for about 5 minutes and for some reason wasn't nobody on the platform but me. My feet seems like they was glued to the ground and I couldn't move, but I manage to walk again made it down the steps. Now I know why they started running, there was at least ten police officers on top of some dude who I think apparently jump the rail, I walk pass the commotion seen my bus and jump on, I didn't want to see dude fuck-up like that, but in my mind I was thinking "Thank you homie whoever you was".

I made it to Uncle Odtis house around 8:00, Sam seems like either he just went to sleep or haven't had any when he open the door and let me in. He said how you get here? I said the bus, He said damn nigga ya bucking aint ya? I said it's all good, didn't tell him what happen at the train station cause I didn't want him to worry, so I kelt it to myself. He said so you got that fa me, I said the whole ten he said that's what's up, so how much you gonna charge me? I said man you know how we do it, just give me what you think is reasonable, I know you aint gonna get over on me. He said aight my man let me go and count up this paper fa ya and I'll be right back, sit down somewhere, I'll be a minute. I said aight, he took the bag and walk in the back room.

He came back like ten minutes later, handed me to two thick envelopes and said that's 15,000, I was finto protest cause I was just gonna charge him 10, but he put his hand and was like don't worry about it, "You know you my lil-nigga, come on I take you back to the train station, "I said preciate ya a lot Sam" He smile and said I know you do, so don't trip, you earn it! nothing else wasn't said until we got to the train station, he said yo yall ever hear anything on ya cousin, "I said knall not yet" He said "well if yall need anything else just let me know aight" I said aight thats whats up" Then he said "Oh I'll need the same thing again in a couple days, you got me? I said all the time" he said "Thats whats up I got out the car and started walking in, he rolled down his window and said yo Boogie, buy yaself a car nigga and stop riding this bus, if you need help finding one come halla at me. "I said I aight Sam I will." I knew he was right, I knew I took a chance today, but tomorrow Sam will be seeing me and I will be purchasing me a car.

CHAPTER SEVENTEEN

"One way in, One way out" . . . .

There is only one way in and one way out and that is, "hell or jail".

25% make it to see better days, 35% don't make it at all,

10% will turn informate<stop snitching> and the other 30% will whined

Up incarcerated. That's just how the game goes. No ifs, ands buts about it, because coma is a muthafucka; just always believe that . . . .

Thoughts of Casey Holmes

W HEN I GOT OFF THE bus where the hotel was, I ran across the street to the store and bought a couple of blunts and a orange juice, with a couple boxes of lemon heads. I walk out the store headed back toward the room, when I got there I notice Red car wasn't there, so I guess him and my brother would be back later. I slid the key in the door and open it, all the lights was off, but the TV was on. I walk pass the bed and Brandon was still sleeping. I said "Yo Brandon, get ya ass up nigga, ya gonna sleep all day". He didn't move. I walk to the bathroom and took a piss, took the envelopes out and counted out 10,000, put tht in one envelop and put the rest in another envelope and put in my pocket. I didn't have to count it, if Sam told me he gave me 15,000 I knew how much I had for myself. I walk back toward the bed, Brandon still haven't move, I said "Yo B" man get up bro, I need to talk to ya, still no movement. I said damn man you and Red must've had a long night. I grab the cover and toss them back to find my brother with a single shot to his head, I couldn't move, I couldn't breathe, I couldn't even think, I just layed my head on his chest grabbing him and started crying. I think I stayed like that for about an hour, I couldn't think for a minute talking to my brother like he probably could hear, but I knew he couldn't. Who did this to you, but the first name that pop in my head was Red. I gonna kill that mutherfucker with sobs of pain and furry, I finally made my way to my feet. I look around the room, close my eyes and prayed that this was a dream, when I open my eyes I knew it wasn't Brandon was dead, more tears started running down my cheeks. I knew I couldn't stay here with him and call the police, I knew they woulda lock me up until they investigation was over, so I got to call them from somewhere else, but at the time my mind was on revenge. I was feeling like someone just stuck me in my heart with a butcher knife, but I had to leave and call the police. I check the room over whipping everything down I touch, went back to my brother one more time, kiss him on the cheek and said I'm gonna get that nigga bro, may you rest in peace." I walk out the room with everything I brought with me, wipe both side of the door, walk back across the street and got on the payphone. "911" the voice said on the other, I had to manage with all my power to talk calm, I said I think someone been shot, I heard a shot at the Red Roof Inn on Northside drive in the room 210" The voice said "and who am I speaking with" I said "please hurry" and hung up. I wipe the phone down, I they would find out that the call came from here and the will be checking for fingerprints. I guess luck was on my side cause when I turn around there was a cab getting gas. I said "Are you working" he look me up and down and said "No I'm just getting off" I thought to myself "I can't stand these scary ass cab driver down here, it aint like New York that you can just wave one of these mutherfucker down, Na'll you got to call and wait for about a hour or two, to get to where you going, but in the dirty South that's how it is, but its ways to get around this shit. I reach in my pocket, I don't know what he thought I was finta rob him or what, but he protest I don't have nothing, I don't have any money" I said "good" pull out a roll of hundreds and slid him one and said "Oakley City please and I need to get there now" he said "no problem sir" I thought to myself "this mutherfucker, but I brush it off and slid in the back seat, then we drove away, just in time cause the police was just pulling in. I glance back for just a second to see about ten cars pilling in the hotel parking lot and two cars drove up to the payphone at the store as we was getting on the highway.

I made it to Sam, he open the door, he said damn nigga I still got more left, I not ready yet" My head was down, he walk me into the house, wasn't nobody around yet, thank God, he said "what's wrong Boogie" I said "he's dead, he's dead "with tears and shaky shoulder he said "who Boogie who" I said "Brandon" then he grab me and held me close, my head was lean on his chest and he was crying cause I felt his tears coming down on my head. He pulled me back and said "Boogie" I look at him, he had so much rage in his eyes and in his voice he said "Tell me what happen". I did, I told him how I found him and everything I did and who was the main suspect on my list. He agreed and said "Red gonna pay for this" he said "do ya mama know" I said "I didn't have the courage to tell her" Sam jump on the phone and was talking to someone furiously telling him what happen. He hung up came back and said Yo Uncle Odtis on his way back he'll be here sometime tonight, he told me to keep you here "I said" I'm gonna kill that nigga, um gonna kill him Sam, um gonna kill him "Sam just nodded and said "I know"

From all the tears, frustration and pain, I doze off in a deep sleep. I was dreaming bout Brandon at first, then I seen myself in the woods the only place that felt safe, the only place I felt peace, the only place I felt at home. I seen myself running, jumping over falling down trees and ducking under limbs, sweating furiously, ducking and dodging every osical that I come face to face with. I was breathing hard but did not stop just ran and ran, telling myself mother nature aint got shit on me, I am nature, but why am I running anyway? What is um running from? Is someone or something ather me? I glance back without even stopping but didn't see nothing, but a shadow, I was thinking what fuck, I knew it was something or someone and whatever it was it was gaining speed. I wasn't scared, I mean what to be scared of, it aint nothing but a shadow I was telling myself, but who shadow? I thought as I kelp running still maneuvering though the woods, nothing couldn't get in my way, telling myself "mother nature aint got shit on me, I am nature. The shadow got closer and closer, I could feel whatever chasing me breathing on my neck, I didn't dare turn around not knowing what it was or who I kelp running, still telling myself "Mother nature aint got shit on me, I am nature" I ran and ran, then all of a sudden, out of nowhere I was push so hard in my back, it felt like two 500lb linebacker running into me. I fell hard right on my face and chest and knock out all my wind, when the impact emerge again, I thought a sumo wrestler just jump on my back, whatever or whoever just broke my back, with one swift motion I was now laying on my back, the shadow cover over me, I couldn't move, it went from day to night with a blink of a eye, I force myself a swing with my fist, but didn't hit nothing, then the face of the shadow emerge, at first it was still shadowy and dark, then it came closer to my face, now we are nose to nose it was Red, he had horns like the devil poking out his head, fire was coming out of his eyes and his teeth reminded me of that clown that played in the Stevin King movie "It", with saliva coming from his mouth he said "Your next muthafucka" I swung hitting him with a quick upper cut in his chin, then I woke up, seeing my Uncle Odtis rubbing his chin, he said "Damn nigga, you almost knock me out", with a grin on his face. I was soaking in sweat and still confuse and daze from the nightmare. I look up at him and he look at me with his arms out, I ran straight in them and we both started crying, it helped me out a lot cause soon as I hug him I felt the fatherly love and protection I never had before in my life.

The following day the moods of my family got more intense, when the detective call my mom and told her, her son has been brutally murder, she had a stroke and was now hospitalize, Sam told me, when he went over last night to check on her and was finta break the news, she was already had fell out, he came just in time to rush her to Grady Memoria, the doctor said it was a minor stroke, but if he wouldn't got there when he did she probably would have died. I had to keep my composure for now, I couldn't lose my mind, I was on a mission and that mission was Red.

Uncle Odtis and Sam already been around to the hood on Demark St. asking there sources have they seen Red around, but nobody has, but we came up on some info, when somebody a female who strip at Booty Tap a clubs in Atlanta that she seen Red a couple nights in a row, spending big money, buying up the bar and all the hoes, practically he was making it rain with cash until he got drunk enough and stumble out, but he came back the next night and did it again. She said the second night she even ask him, where Brandon at cause she knew they was tight and all, but she said he was already drunk, so she didn't think nothing of it when he said "Bitch fuck that nigga, ya worried bout the wrong thing, now shut up and shake that ass bitch" she brush it off and continue to get his money, she said he gave a $200 tip before he left and said he'll be back tonight. "The plan is that we gonna wait for my source to call me tonight when she see him, then we gonna go and wait for him to come out "Uncle Odtis told us, so we waited.

It was a hour pass midnight when Uncle Odtis receive the call. "Hello" he said into the phone. Sam and I waited and anticipated while Uncle Odtis talk "um huh, um huh fashow" he hung up. He look at Sam and me, he said "Shorty said he been there since 11:00 and he already real washed, spending big bread "Sam ran to the back room, came back with a black bag, Uncle Odtis said "you got everything" Sam said you already know. "They both look at me, Uncle Odtis knoded his head to Sam, then Sam went out the door, to get the car ready. Uncle Odtis said Boogie, ya sure you up to this "I look him dead in the eyes and said "Um gonna kill um and in my heart I knew I was. Uncle Odtis said "let's go then my nig". We walk out the house, jump in the car and rode out.

We pulled up to the parking lot, back in a park, turn off the head light and waited. We knew he was still inside cause his caprice was still outside. It was 2:45 we knew the spot close up bout 5:00, but usually the big spenders try to leave before the crowd come out, so we was hoping Red would. Rage was building up in me, thinking about my brother, then I thought about my moma, then fury of angry miss with hated was in my eyes a tear rolled down my cheek. I just wanted to go right in the club and shoot that nigga on the spot and wait for the police, but then I thought about my moma again and knew that would surly kill her, if she loses her last son, over some bullshit, so I had to be wise. I was sitting up front with Sam and Uncle Odtis in the back, it was now 3:30, the longer we waited the madder I got. I had a 357 revolver snub nose, "No evidence, no case" is what I always say. "This nigga need to come on. I thought to myself. "Where the fuck is this nigga" 3:50 and God just answer my prayers. I looked up and Red was coming out the door staggering. I open the door and was getting out, but Uncle Odtis grab my shoulder pulling me back in. I said what the fuck man he said not now, I said "aint nobody out here" he said "The streets is always watching, be patient" By then he done jump in the car and was pulling ou the parking lot. Uncle Odtis told Sam "You know what to do. We got right behind him and followed him. I said "damn Uncle Odtis, I could have got his punk ass" he said "Boogie I know ya mad right now, so um gonna excuse, but trust me nigga, I know what I'm talking about, just be patience aight." Aight I said, but still breathing hard from the adrenaline rush that built up in me. I settle back in my seat, 357 still tight in my fist, waiting for the car in front of me to stop. Telling myself, he just doesn't know, he's a dead man walking.

We pulled off the highway tailing the caprice and was going the same way we usually go to Uncle Odtis house I was thinking where in the hell this nigga going? We pulled up to the mortuary around the corning from the gambling house, the caprice rolled to the back of the mortuary, I was thinking out loud to myself. "What the fuck this nigga doing? My hand tightens around the 357 as both cars stop. I jump out so fast; I heard Uncle Odtis said Boogie!!! But it was too late, couldn't anybody stop me now, I was determined to kill this nigga, I was on a mission and that mission wasn't failure. I went around as fast as I could, gun aim and ahead of me, then the driving side door came open. My finger was tight around the trigger, when big man jump out and said "hold on man, hold on" by then Uncle Odtis and Sam was standing behind me. Uncle Odtis said "Boogie meet Bobby," I said what the fuck going on, where the fuck is Red" Bobby said look in the back seat" I open the door still with my pistol drown and what I seen was Red body slump on the floor. I knew he was dead because his head was facing me but his back was to me. Bobby done twisted and broke his neck all the way. What one quick switch motion Bobby grab him, put Red on his shoulder and carried the limp lifeless body in the back door of the mortuary. Still stun Uncle Odtis grab my arm and said "come on Boogie". We followed Bobby inside pass open caskets some filled with bodies already. We walk in another room, there was a gig oven and though the gate I can see fire blazing, it made the whole room hot and stuffy. Bobby layed Red body on a steel plaque form, open the gate to the oven, then pulled a level, the plaque form with Red body started to move inward. Uncle Odtis came and stood beside me and said "Boogie I'm sorry, but I couldn't let ya moma loose her last boy to evidence or jail". I said I know Uncle Odtis said it's over now, now Brandon can rest in peace. Still gripping the 357 I aimed it at Red Body and shot him 8 times wishing the revolver held more. I said now I can Rest in Peace we watch in silence as Red body went into the gate and burn. I threw the 357 in there with him, then Uncle Odtis, Sam and I turn around and left to let Bobby do what he do best being the clean up man. Walking out the door Bobby started laughing and it gave all of us a chill. Uncle Odtis said Sam take that caprice and let them boys around the corner strip that muthafucka down, tell them we don't want it to be seen again, we will meet you back at the house. Now let's get the fuck up out of here. I jump in with Uncle Odtis, Sam jump in the caprice, then we rolled out in the early morning mist.

Everybody deserves a second chance, but whatever you make of it will be

All on you. You can continue to live and do the same things and stay

In the same bind and situation or you can change your mind, your

Ways; to pursue and fulfill the goals you was set out to achieve,

To: All those haters out there in the worked; who don't have nothing

Better else to do with their lives, but to try to make other people lives

Miserable in any kind of way; just remember these 5 words

That will maybe help yall stop hating on other's and each other, so Don't
Hate Me, Hate Yourself> . . . .

Thoughts of Casey Holmes

CHAPTER EIGHTEEN

"A Second Chance"....

W E RODE PASS UNCLE ODTIS, I didn't ask where we was going, I had a feeling I already knew. We park in the parking garage next door and go out the car and walk in Grady Memorial Hospital. Uncle Odtis already knew where mama was so I followed him up a elevator, around a couple of corners and there I was standing in the door way of the most beautiful lady in the world my mama. I just stood there for a moment, couldn't get myself to step over that thresh hole. There wasn't no lights on but the TV. My moma was laying there seems to be sleeping, but I noticed all the tubes and machines she was hook up to, tears started to rush down my cheek. I was thinking to myself, damn I wish I could go back and shoot Red a couple more times, but I knew that wasn't gonna happen, he was burning in hell before we even left. I stared around the room for a minute; there was a person slash in one of the chairs sleeping, well it looks like they was trying to anyway. I wipe away my tears so I could see clearer. I said Ebony, she look up and ran to the door and gave me a hug and we both started crying in each other arms, she said Boogie where you been, we haven't seen each other in a while, but the love was there, she said "mama been worry sick bout you, you heard bout Brandon right" I said Yea, then we started crying some more, then Uncle Odtis came up and said "Ebony, let ya brother go in alone, she just nodded and her and Uncle walk away. I finally made my way to the side of the bed. I grab her hand and said "Moma, moma are you awake" she didn't move, so I said "well if you can hear me, this Boogie and I just want to tell you "I'm sorry for making ya worry and I love you, very much, her hand grip mines as tight as she could with her other hand she signaled for me to lean in closer, her voice was harsh, but soft with love she said "Boogie I love you too" a tear ran down her cheek, then she doze back off to sleep. I kiss her forehead, then left the room looking back one more time at the most beautiful woman in the world my moma.

The funeral for my brother was held in the streets of Atlanta, from Oakland City; pass the West-End, though the heart of Downtown underground, to the cemetery, off of Boulevard, where we held the sermon and the burial. My Uncle Odtis made it special for us. Brandon was carried all the way on the back of a two white horse carriage. It was a nice service. People came from all over to pay their respects to one of the realist nigga you would ever known. The tomb stone read:

In the memory of Brandon Jenkins A.K.A GHOST

May you rest in peace and your spirit continues to bless us with your love.

1978-1997

TWO WEEKS LATER UNCLE ODTIS took me, moma and Ebony on a vacation to Jamaica, it was so nice and sunny, we all enjoyed ourselves and was so thankful to be able to spend some time with each other. I was walking on the beach just thinking to myself and was wondering what I would do when I get back home? Uncle Odtis enteruped my thinking it seems like he always know what I be thinking about, he said "You thinking bout what you gonna do when you get home", I said "yea", he said Don't think to hard you might bust a brain cell" I started laughing he said "don't worry ya self about it, ya gonna be ok. I got something in mind fa ya," I said "what" cause I was curious he said "Just be ready to make a change, just look at it as a second chance to get ya self straight" to be off the streets and be able to take care of ya moma and sister "I said aight, thats whats up" he said "Now enjoy ya vacation" he pass pass me a big ass pliff he said "smoke some of this Jamaica" I took the pliff whatever he called it, fired it up, while walking on the beach into the sunset.

Cash money can bring the good and the bad of a person.

The color I called Greedy Green can change a person

Whole demeanor and character without a person

Even knowing it. this is what it is; when it comes down to cash, color and character; just beware of your surrounding because it can kill you and it can break you, if not wise, focus or careful.

Money comes and goes, but life is more valuable . . . .

Thoughts of Casey Holmes

CHAPTER NINETEEN

"Cash, Color & Characters"....

WHEN WE GOT BACK IN town, things were as usual in the hood and at the gambling house, With the 15,000 I had spent 10 of it to finally get my moma and sister out of the hood. I bought my moma a house in Stone Mountain but 2 years later she died of a massive stroke that took her life. Now Ebony and my moma best friend Sara live there, I go by there on occasions but not much, I try to let the ladies have their privacy and snce I always been on my own, I couldn't bare been there any way. I got me a house around the corner though just to make sure nobody fuck with them and if they do need me I'll be close by. My cousin Rollin got charge with manslaughter and was sent to 5 years in prison, I go and keep money on his books and write every so often, but he call most of the time, he never told the police anything about me. Greg got bout 2 years left, he's doing ok he as hurt about Brandon, but crush about his wife and my moma Joanna. Egg I talk to a lot more now, we kicked and go out, he still one of the fattest freshest nigga I know. Pete died in a car accident, they say when they found him he had a blunt in his mouth. Bobby the clean up man still cleaning up everybody messes. Sam still running the gambling house and keeping it live and jumping. Uncle Odtis went back to where he was and not planning on coming back until Greg gets out, before he left he said "Always listen to your first instinct." And my Uncle Odtis put me second in charge of the gambling house, so I wouldn't have to be on the streets much. We planning to relocate soon, but we decided to wait to Greg get out and Uncle Odtis come back. Can't wait to Odtis, Greg and Rollin touch back down, but until then um gonna continue to, Get Money!!!!!

TO BE CONTINUE

S TAY TUNE TO THE NEXT adventure to come when Greg and Rollin gets release from prison, Odtis makes his way back home, Sam step up his game and running a strip club, Ebony helps out Sam by dancing and keeping the other dancers in check and Joe Jr. finds his way in the system doing a little time, but when these heads all come together, some may bump alone the way, but they realize they have the same goals, getting that money and realize with their minds, they can take over the streets of the Dirty South in:

THE
AMERICAN
WAY II